The Lily Pickle Band Book

"Fall in," yells Mr Kendal.

And little Stella Green, who hasn't stopped marching yet behind Mr Kendal's mac, she straight away throws herself into the river. Mr Kendal looks at her, and his best mac, then he looks at me, and my wet feet, and he says, "I'm a broken man, Mrs W. A broken man."

And this is only the beginning of Mr Kendal's efforts to start up a children's band. Most of its members, from old Mavis Jarvis (otherwise known as Poison Ivy) down to little Stella and her dog, seem to have a knack of making this as difficult for him as possible – without even trying.

"Gwen Grant's colourful characters are larger than life, her stories are taller than most, and her style is rough-edged, colloquial and very, very funny."
The Signal Review of Children's Books

D1149411

Other titles in Fontana Young Lions

The Lily Pickle Band Book

GWEN GRANT

Illustrated by Margaret Chamberlain

Fontana Young Lions

First published in Great Britain 1982
by William Heinemann Ltd
First published in Fontana Young Lions 1983
8 Grafton Street, London W1X 3LA
Third impression June 1987

Fontana Young Lions is an imprint of
Fontana Paperbacks, part of
the Collins Publishing Group

Copyright © Gwen Grant 1982

Printed in Great Britain by
William Collins Sons & Co. Ltd, Glasgow

For my sister, Glenda

Contents

1

Mr Kendal thinks he has a good idea

I am writing this story under a false name as I do not want anyone to know it is me that has written it.

In some countries, when they find a dead body, unless it has its name written on the soles of its feet or in blue ink on its arm – and that doesn't happen very often, I can tell you – they call these bodies John Doe or Jane Doe, depending on whether it's a lass or a lad, you know.

Well, I am going to sign this 'Jane Doe' because, if I do not, then I shall be as dead as any dead body myself when certain people have read it.

The most certain person of all would be Mavis Jarvis, who is about twelve feet tall, twelve feet wide and a hundred feet thick in the head. You could spit rivets at her head and she wouldn't even notice them going in, she's that thick.

E. Harris says Mavis J. was made out of a Do-It-Yourself kit from Mackies Ironmongers.

"She don't feel rivets going in," he says, "because her head's full of 'em already."

I don't know about that. I'm willing to believe it though. All I do know is that they reckon when she was a baby, people used to look in her pram, go cross-eyed and hand her a banana.

Well, I am halfway between twelve and thirteen years old. My Gran says she is halfway to heaven but she is very old with white hair and knows a lot.

I have got one Gran and one Mam and no Dad to speak of. The reason we don't speak of him is because he came into the kitchen one night when I was six years old and said to my Mam, "This is the end. I am going to seek my fortune." And he went to work at the dog food factory which closed down two weeks later.

My Mam said it was the factory's own fault for taking my Dad on.

"Never could keep anything, he couldn't," she says, and then my Dad went away and nobody's heard from him since.

I says to my Gran, "What were my Dad like, Gran?" and she says, "I'm saying nothing. All I ask you to remember is that if I hadn't been there, you'd have been answering to Honolulu Baby by now."

"Honolulu Baby?" I says and my Gran nods her head and goes, "Your Mam and Dad went to the pictures a week before you was born and saw this lass wearing nothing but a blade of grass and a smile and she was called Honolulu Baby. Your Dad thought that was a very good name." And Gran snorted and said I wasn't to bring the subject up again if I didn't mind because, speaking for herself, she was certain sure said subject would turn up one day of his own accord.

Well, I reckon a Dad as could call a person Honolulu Baby when they live round here is more trouble than he's worth.

Where I live is a mining town right on the far north tip of Nottinghamshire and if you tell people you live here, they go, "Oh yes. Stagecoach still running there, is it?" and think they are very funny which they are not.

This story I'm writing though is about our band. I thought I'd better write down about our band before I forget.

Mavis Jarvis had a part in the school play last Christmas as the front end of the horse carrying Prince Charming with his plastic shoe to old Cinderella there in the kitchen. She forgot to put the horse's head on when she went on the stage but it didn't make any difference. Two little kids at the front still gave her a carrot each.

Anyway, as I was saying. This story is really about our band which is called The Workton Whistler's Children's Jazz Band and Mr Kendal from Rat-Trap House, which is really the second block of flats where we all live, he's running it.

One day he gets all the kids and their Mams and Dads together and he says, "Now then, I want all them kids who 'asn't got nowt better to do to come to the Palace Gardens tonight." Then he sucks his breath in through his teeth till he whistles, wheee, he goes and looks at the Mams and Dads and says, "Band, you know," and winks with his left eye.

All the Mams and Dads say, "Right," and, "Yers, I should think so," and that's that.

Palace Gardens is a mucky great field with a scout hut on it, two goal posts and a river.

Everybody goes there at night anyway.

So, this night, comes seven o'clock and there's Mr Kendal on the field and he's shouting, "Now come on, you lot. Let's get this show on the road," and we all look round for the show and find out that we're IT. We're the show.

It turns out then that Mr Kendal and Mrs Warren, from next door to us, they're going to make us into a band that plays and marches at the same time.

Mrs Warren says, "Don't you think that's a bit ambitious, Mr Kendal? Playing and marching at the same time?" But Mr Kendal shakes his head and says, "What! They don't know what they can do till they try," and tells us how, when he was in the Army, he marched five days and five nights carrying his wounded pal.

I happen to know his wounded pal was an ant with a broken leg in a matchbox.

Mr Kendal told me so but he didn't tell any of the others.

I says to him, "How did you know it had got a broken leg, Mr Kendal?" because ants aren't very big so as you can have a look.

Mr Kendal tapped his nose with his finger and whispers, "It 'obbled when it walked."

I don't know what to think about that. None of the ants I've ever seen hobble but then, perhaps none of them had a broken leg.

Anyway, Mr Kendal gets us all together in the middle of the field and makes us stand in rows and E. Harris takes one look at this band and he says to Mr Kendal, "You ought to call it The Workton Wellies," which Mr Kendal didn't find very funny at all, but I looked round and there were eight of us in wellies and only thirteen in the band.

This band though is different from any other band I've ever heard about because you don't have to know how to play anything at all to be in it.

All you have to do to join is nod.

You nod when Mr Kendal says, "Who wants to play the kazoo?" You nod when he says, "And who wants to play the drums?" And you nod when he says, "And what about these here tambourines?"

Before you know where we are, there we are. A band. The Workton Whistler's Children's Jazz Band.

Mrs Warren shouts, "Now then. Who's going to be the girl who leads the band?" because even though there are lads in these bands, the leader always has to be a girl.

14

Before Mrs W. can draw another breath in order not to choke to death you know who's there, don't you, up at the front, pushing her nasty, piggy, little nose up against Mrs Warren's purple cardigan.

"Me," she says, and Mavis the Mandrake has struck again.

It says in the dictionary that mandrake is "a poisonous plant . . . thought to resemble human form and to shriek when plucked."

Well, that is very true of Mavis Jarvis, particularly the poisonous bit and she does only look a bit like a human being as well and you have to look hard to see even that. Unless, of course, they mean a monkey when they say "human form". Then you can see the likeness at a glance.

Anyway, there she is, going, "I'll lead the band. I'll lead the band."

"Why," says Mrs Warren. "It is nice to see you so keen, Mavis," and she looks round to see if anybody else wants to lead the band and there's Karen Green with her hand in the air.

"I'd like to lead the band as well," says Karen.

Mrs Warren goes, "Well," tut tut. "Two of you." And E. Harris says, "They're very quick these grown-ups, aren't they?" and Mr Kendal hears him and says, "Now then, don't let's have any of your cheek round here, my son."

So, Mrs Warren says, "Well, the thing is, girls, whoever leads the band has to be very good at tossing this stick up in the air and catching it and then tossing it up again. Not to mention twirling it round and round, all without dropping it and particularly without dropping it onto somebody's head."

Everybody thinks about this for a bit and I says to E. Harris, "What if you threw that stick up and it never came down again?" And E. Harris, he says, "Where is there for it to go in the sky?" And he looks up and goes on, "If you'd just look up, like I'm doing, you'd see the sky is empty."

"I know it's empty now," I says, "but what if God got fed up with people chucking their sticks in the air and he put his hand down and whipped one up to heaven?"

"Something like that happened when me and my rock group E. H. and the Dead Beats were practising in the school hall," E. Harris said. "Only it weren't the hand of God, it was the hand of the headmaster plucked our drumsticks out of thin air. Blinking hand like a rhubarb leaf, he had as well, and he wouldn't give us our sticks back no how. 'Terrible racket' he says, and puts them in his desk and there they are to this day."

E. Harris is in a band already. He has this rock group and they wear royal blue suits with black velvet collars and sequins round the cuffs, bootlace ties and a lot of scent. You can smell them a mile off and, if you try and stand near them, you keel over in a dead faint.

E. Harris says that is because they are the greatest but it's really because they're the smelliest.

He asked me once if I'd go along and scream for them so I did and this bloke chucked them out because he said they were frightening all the little kids.

E. Harris wouldn't speak to me for about a month.

Then he says, "You were supposed to scream as if you liked us, not as if you'd just come face to face with Dracula."

I says to him, "Well, it weren't my fault. I was looking at you at the time."

Anyway, I thought I wouldn't put up my hand to lead the band in case the Hand of God came down and scooped me up instead.

Mavis Jarvis, though, she stuck her chest out and says, "I can do it, Mrs Warren. I can."

Then Karen Green, who can get very nasty when she wants to, she shoves old Mavis out of the way and goes, "And I can do it as well, Mrs Warren."

17

In the end Mrs Warren says, "Well, we shall just have to have a competition to decide, that's all." And she gives Mavis and Karen a stick each and tells them they've got half an hour to practise in.

"Go to the far side of the field out of harm's way," she says, "and in thirty minutes, we'll see who's best. Whoever's the best gets to lead the band," and she smiles. The only one who does. "I think that's fair, girls, isn't it?" she goes.

We're all going nudge nudge by now because although Mrs Warren thinks it's fair, we all know Mavis Jarvis.

Mr Kendal played war when he turned round and saw all his band vanishing over the field.

"Where you lot going?" he shouts, and somebody tells him we're going to watch Mavis Jarvis and Karen Green practising to be the leader of the band.

"Oh well," Mr Kendal says. "It was time for a break, anyhow." And he starts sorting out all his combs and bits of newspaper.

Trouble is, see, we haven't actually got any kazoos and things.

Mr Kendal says, "We'll just have to make do till we can afford some instruments. Them kazoos sound just like a comb and a bit of newspaper does, and we can use old tin plates

18

for the cymbals." And then he stops and says, "We're going to have to raise some money, I can see that coming."

By the time we get to the corner of the field, Karen Green is beginning to look a bit pink because these sticks Mrs Warren's given them, they're like pit props.

Mavis J. was all right. She's built like a pit prop herself. She even looks like one. She was tossing her stick around as if it were a match.

Then she starts marching up and down like Mrs Warren showed her, throwing this stick in the air.

The first time she throws it up, she stands there grinning waiting for it to come down and E. Harris, me and Karen Green started running but this stick got us and it felled all of E. H., all of me, except for one foot, which was already on the ground anyway, and half of Karen Green. The other half of her was stood there yelling and screaming at Mavis J.

"Oops, sorry," says old M. and laughs her stupid head off.

Then Karen gets to have a go and she starts marching and we're all whistling 'The Grand Old Duke of York', except Mavis J. that is, she's sneering, and Karen just gets to where they're marching down again when she throws the stick as high as she can, catches it, twirls it round three times and then clumps Mavis Jarvis across the back of the legs with it.

Well, I must say that was the best part of the night. If every band night's going to be this good, I shan't miss one.

E. Harris, he takes one look at Karen Green and Mavis Jarvis with two pit props fighting it out between them and he says, "Well, I'm not going in no band with them telegraph poles in it, I can tell you that for nothing." But Mr Kendal, he says, "They're not supposed to knock folk to the ground." And he tells Mavis and Karen they'd better behave else they're out on their ears and then he turns round and says to me, "Here, you can lead the band."

Then he tells Karen and Mavis J. they'd better stop practising pretty darn quick while he's still got some band left, because everybody's on the ground holding their legs and arms and bits of their bodies and they're all moaning and groaning because of where these pit props have hit them.

Well, old Mavis doesn't like that at all and she throws her stick up and then marches off and leaves it to come down all on its own, which wasn't very clever, because it came down on top of old Mavis herself.

I thought E. Harris was having a heart attack because after one look at Mavis Jarvis flat on her back with this stick lying across her, he falls to the ground going erk, erk, erk. I had to bash him on the back to stop him choking. He didn't stop laughing for an hour.

He wasn't on his own, either. Three quarters of the band were down there with him.

Mr Kendal looks at them and then at Mavis and he says, "I can just see what kind of a band this is going to be." Then that lot who're Mavis Ug's pals, they go over and help her up and pick this stick up and next minute they're beating everybody round the head with it.

Mr Kendal and Mrs Warren say, "We're not having that," and they stop all the fighting, which was a shame as we were just getting going. Then Mr Kendal says, "Well, I think that's it for tonight and Lily Pickle here, she's the band leader."

That's my real name, Lily Pickle. Everybody calls me Piccalilli. They think they're so funny.

All I think is, what would have happened if I'd been called Honolulu Baby?

2

Practice makes perfect sometimes

Well, I was going to write about the band under a different name but now I've written my own name down, so that's that.

When I told my Gran about it, she said, "I should just think you have put it under your own name, Lily. There was never anything written that was worth reading without a proper name signed to it."

Before we broke up last time, Mr Kendal says, "Now then, we're a bit short of sticks, so I want anybody who's got a spare brush handle to bring it with them." When we got there tonight, there's Michelle Parish walking up the road dragging her Mam's old vacuum cleaner.

I says to her, "Are you sure Mr Kendal wants that?" and Michelle she says, "Well, my Mam hadn't got a brush handle but she said this was the next best thing, see." When we got to the field, Michelle pulls this old cleaner up to Mr Kendal and he looks at it and then he looks at her and he says, "You've not taken up ploughing, Michelle, have you?" and when we look round, there's this field all chewed up just as if a plough's been there.

Michelle says, "I brought this instead of a brush handle, Mr Kendal," and Mr Kendal strokes his chin and shuts his eyes a bit and then he says, "Yes, well. It's for throwing up in the air, you see, Michelle. You can't really do that with a vacuum cleaner, can you?" and old Mavis Jarvis, she leaps forward and shouts, "You can, Mr Kendal, you can," and she grabs this cleaner off Michelle and tosses it up in the air as if it's a drinking straw.

No wonder all the bullets missed Mr Kendal in the war. You should have seen how fast he moved. He was a hundred yards up that field before you could blink.

Mavis J. she just steps out of the way and this vacuum cleaner comes down on Stella Green's dog's tail and he's a dog who never barks first. He always bites and then barks.

Karen Green, she says he's the best guard dog in the flats. He must be. He won't even let Karen Green's Dad get in their flat because he doesn't like men and Mavis Jarvis.

They call him Tiny and he's about as big as a double decker bus. Well, old Tiny, he hops around howling his head off and little Stella Green, who is five years old and wants to be in the band as well, she kneels down and says, "It did it, doggie," and points to Mavis J.

Stella always calls Mavis *It*, and Mavis says to her, "Why don't you go and play with the trains," and points to the railway lines but Stella's got more sense than that.

Anyway, this dog, he sort of freezes with his nose pointing in the air, then he lifts one of his paws and jumps straight at Mavis J. and sends her flying.

By the time Mr Kendal gets back, Tiny's got Mavis pinned down with a paw on each shoulder. Mavis isn't scared though. She's lying there with Tiny's nose about a quarter of an inch from hers and his teeth are all dribbling spit on her neck and she's shouting, "Gerroff, you stupid dog. Gerroff," and Tiny's crouched there wondering which is the best bit to bite first.

Mr Kendal nearly had a fit. "Get up, girl," he shouts. "This is supposed to be a band, not a dog training school," and he pulls old Tiny away with his collar.

Stella Green, she says, "Mister. Mister. Can I be in the band, can I?" and Mr Kendal says, "You're too young, Stella," but Mrs Warren, she says, "They have them younger than that, Mr Kendal. They have them as mascots and they walk behind the band's banner."

"At five years of age?" Mr Kendal says and Mrs Warren nods.

So Mr Kendal thinks about this for a bit and then he says to Stella, "All right, Stella. You can be in the band. You can be the mascot. But you've got to bring us luck, mind."

Stella goes bright red and she says, "I will, Mr Kendal. I will." Then Mr Kendal looks at me and he says, "Have you been practising marching?" and I say, "Yes."

"Throwing a stick in the air at the same time?" he goes on and I nod and say, "Yes," and E. Harris, he says, "She broke the Co-op window doing that and her Mam's got to pay for it at fifty pence a week."

Mr Kendal says, "Whatever happened?" and I told him.

"The stick went one way, Mr K. and I went another."

This is what happens, you see, when you throw things in the air.

Mr Kendal sighed and then he shouts, "All right. All right. Line up," and so we all line up except Stella Green. She sat down because she said her legs were tired.

Mrs Warren says to her, "You can't be a mascot with tired legs, Stella," so Stella jumps up and says her legs aren't tired any more, and old Mavis J., who's picked herself up off the ground, she says, "You're the tattiest mascot I've ever seen," and Karen, she smacks Mavis straight in the mouth.

Mr Kendal's shouting, "Now then, you lasses. Come on. Pack it in. Pack it in, I tell you." And he's trying to pull them apart and when he finally does, Karen Green's just about frothing at the mouth and her left eye, where Mavis J. put her fist, it's almost shut.

Mavis Jarvis is standing there with blood pouring out of her lip where Karen hit her and she's sort of pawing the ground and tossing her head at the same time.

"Let me at 'er," she's saying. "Let me at 'er." But Mr Kendal gives her his hanky and tells her to wipe the blood away and then he says to Karen, "Put a wet cloth on that eye, Karen, and if there's any more fighting, you're both out of the band."

By the time it was all quiet again, practically the whole night had gone.

It's a pity it hadn't all gone because I could have done without what happened next.

Mr Kendal, he finally gets us all lined up and he puts his mac on a stick and tells Stella Green to walk behind that and pretend it's the band's banner, and then he says, "When I whistle, start marching."

I says to him, "Shall I throw the stick up in the air, as well," and he says, "Yes." So he whistles and we start marching and I throw the stick up and all the band take off down the field.

"All right. All right. Point taken," Mr Kendal roars, and gets them all lined up again. "Never mind the stick," he says to me. "Just march."

So we start again and then Mr Kendal shouts, "Good. Good. Now, left turn," and I can practically feel my eyeballs going round and round like they do in the pin ball machines at the seaside. I think they'll probably drop out in a minute and Mr K., he doesn't care, all he does is shout, "Left, I tell you. Left," and I keep marching and right in front of me is the river and I think, "Cor blimey!" and I march straight into that and Mr Kendal's dancing up and down screaming, "I said left. Left I said," and the rest of the band stand on the bank and cheer.

I don't stop till I get to the other side and then I turn round and Mr Kendal says, "Why?" and I says, "I just get mixed up, Mr Kendal," and all the band's lying about on the grass laughing their stupid heads off, all except Mavis J. that is. She's standing there going, "Ner, ner. Pickled Onion can't tell left from right. Pickled Onion can't tell left from right," and Mr K. goes, "That'll do, Mavis," and when M. J. opens her mouth again, he lifts his finger and says, "I said that'll do," and she shuts up.

Mavis Jarvis has such a big mouth, one of these days she'll open it and astronomers for miles around will go, "Good grief. A new Black Hole."

Then Mr Kendal claps a hand over his eyes and stands there all quiet like you do on Poppy Day when they have the Remembrance Service at the Memorial down by the Library, and then he sort of puts his shoulders back and says, "*Courage, mon ami*," and yells, "Fall in." And little Stella Green, who hasn't stopped marching yet behind Mr Kendal's mac, she straight away throws herself into the water.

I thought Mr Kendal was done for then. He looks at young Stella lying in the river with his best mac floating round her, and then he looks at me and he gets hold of Mrs Warren and he says, "I'm a broken man, Mrs W. A broken man."

Mrs Warren, she says, "There, there, Mr Kendal," and trots down and hauls Stella out of the river and tells her to go straight home and get dried.

Karen, she comes and lifts Stella up with the back of her jumper and Stella goes Erk,

erk, because her jumper's nearly choking her and Karen shakes her and says, "Who's a silly girl?" and lets her drop and Stella starts yelling her head off then.

"Take her home, Karen," Mr Kendal says but Karen won't.

"I'm not taking her home. I'll get a good hiding when my Mam sees her, as it is," and she shakes young Stella again and says to her, "What did you throw yourself in the water for, stupid?" and Stella roars, "Mr Kendal said, 'Fall in'."

Mr Kendal starts saying, "But it doesn't mean . . ." and then he stopped and said to Mrs Warren, "Well, there's only one thing for it, Mrs W. I'll have to take the child home myself." Then he tells the band to practise till he gets back.

Mrs Warren, she says, "No, Mr Kendal. Look, I'll take Stella home and you can get on," and Mr K. says, "Thank you very much, Mrs Warren," and then he yells at us to get in line again.

I notice nobody's bothered about my wet feet.

When we're all in line again, Mr Kendal says to me, "This time you walk away from the river and put this bit of string on your left hand – there," he says, and ties this bit of string round a finger. "When I say 'left', you go the way the string goes. When I say 'right', you go the other way. O.K.?" I nod and say "Yes, Mr Kendal."

"Instruments to mouths," Mr K. shouts and we all put our combs and paper to our mouths. "Blow!" Mr Kendal shouts. "Er, we're playing that there marching song you all know." And he hummed a bit of it and we all said, "Oh, yers," and then we started blowing on our combs and bits of paper and it didn't sound at all bad.

"Well," says Mr Kendal. "We're getting on all right now," and that's when it started to rain.

First of all it was only a little bit but, by the time Mrs Warren got back, it was a bit heavier and she says, "They'll get their death of colds in this," and Mr K. he says, "But we've only just got going." And he shouts, "Instruments to mouths," again and we do. Then he roars, "Blow!" and we all breathe in to breathe out and, the next thing, we're spitting out great soggy chunks of newspaper which the rain has wet through.

Mr Kendal stands listening to his band going, "Yuk!" and, "Spit!" and, "Splutter!" and, "Ain't it 'orrible!" And he says, "All right. All right. Fall out. That's it for tonight."

So we all went home and I was glad.

E. Harris asked me if I wanted to go and hear his group practise because I can dance.

"If you come," he says, "I'll let you dance," so I went.

They've got the Concert Hall in the Old People's Flats to practise in and E. H. has this big piece of card with E. H. and the Dead Beats on it and he props it up in front of the little stage there and then him and his Dead Beats get up with their guitars and drums and they start playing.

They hadn't got any further than the first two chords of 'Rockin' all over' when the Warden comes to the door and shouts, "What a racket. Here, you'll have to be quieter than that," and E. Harris tells her they've got permission.

"I don't care if you've got German Measles," she says. "Keep the noise down."

E. Harris sighs and says to the Dead Beats, who are Gary Smith, "Cool it, Tiger," and Tiger, who is Gary Smith, he says, "Sure thing, Elvis, old friend."

Tiger! Gary Smith weighs about two stone wet through. He's just as tall as a lamp-post and as thin as a piece of cotton. When he's got an apple in his hand, it looks as if somebody's put a knot in his skin.

I says to him, "Do you growl, then?" and he throws one of the drum sticks at me. Very polite they are around here.

E. Harris, he really is called Elvis. His Mam and Dad were big Elvis Presley fans but, when they talk about him now, they don't call him Elvis any more, they call him The King. I says to E. Harris (known as E. Harris because he is tone deaf), "Why do you call him The King?" and he says because E. Presley was the best in the world save one.

"Who's that then?" I asks and E. Harris, he says, "Me."

Then they play a song about some shoes that somebody's going to tread on and E. Harris starts doing the splits. Well, I don't think he meant to do the splits, it's just that he got his legs so wide apart, he couldn't get them back together again.

E. Harris stands there, strumming on his guitar, and you never heard a worse noise in your whole life, until he started singing that was, and his feet kept going further and further apart and E. H. starts looking all worried. Then, he tries to balance on one foot and bring the other foot back where it belongs – on the end of his leg, but this other foot, it's going out and out and, in the end, E. Harris collapses in a big heap with his guitar underneath him and he says, "Blinking heck, what a life," and that's the end of practising for that night.

The only dance I got was with Mr Kendal's old Dad when he came in and put a record on and he dances a dance called the St Bernard's Waltz.

If ever you want to feel really stupid, try doing that with all your mates looking in through the windows.

Mr Kendal's old Dad, he's got false teeth and every time he talked to me, the top set fell down and went click.

I says to him, "You ought to be in our band, Mr K." and he says, "Why?" and I says to him, "Oh, nothing. I just thought you ought to be, that's all," because Mr K's false teeth click in time and that's what that stupid band needs. Somebody to keep us in time.

Well, that's it again.

Mr Kendal says we have to raise some money to buy some proper instruments for the band to play on, so the first thing we're going to do is have a concert.

Grown-ups and everything can be in it.

If Mrs Smith does her impression of a cuckoo falling out of a tree, it should be all right.

She goes, "What does the cuckoo say when it falls out of its nest?" and then she answers herself, "Instead of *Cuckoo*, it goes Cuck-ouch," and falls about laughing and everybody's stood there with their grins all ready and nowhere to put them.

That doesn't stop Mrs Smith though. Boy, and they say kids are stupid.

3

M. J. and the dance of the net curtains

We had the concert last night. Mr Kendal said the band were doing so well, we could do a little tune and a march down the middle of the hall. We all thought that was very good.

He said, "Do you think we could leave the tennis balls at home?" and everybody looked all thoughtful except for E. Harris, he said, "If they leave them tennis balls at home, I'm not coming, for one." So Mr Kendal sighed and said well, perhaps E. H. was right. "We don't want any of the audience carried out unconscious, do we?" he said and laughed a bit, like this, ha ha.

The tennis balls are split and stuck on one end of our sticks because there's three or four of us carrying these sticks now and chucking them up in the air. When one wallops you, it doesn't hurt half so much if it's the end with the tennis ball on it.

Mrs Warren, she says we have to imagine they're the silver tops of beautiful shiny black maces, but it's a bit difficult to imagine that when you've got your Mam's old brush handle in your hand with a tennis ball stuck on top of it. Of course, these grown-ups, there's no end to the things they can imagine.

Mr Kendal for a start, he imagines he can give a concert without the lady from the fish and chip shop being in it.

My Gran laughed when she heard that. She said, "He must have a strong imagination that Mr Kendal." But she said she'd come.

I says to her, "Will my Dad be there, Gran?" and she says, "If he is, he wants star billing. I can just see it now, 'Alan. Escape Artiste Extra-Ordinary' (Alan's my Dad). Mr Kendal'll be able to go on and say, "Now you see him, now you don't." But my Gran didn't laugh at that. Neither did I.

Before the concert started last night, we had a quick march down the hall and back and it was very good. Nobody fell down and nobody got clobbered either.

Mr Kendal brought his front room curtains to use for the front of the stage and Mrs Warren said she'd take the chance to wash and iron them for him if he wanted.

Mr Kendal said, "Well, that's very nice of you, Mrs W." and Mrs Warren went all pink.

E. H. he watches all this and he goes nudge nudge. "See them," he says, "be going out with each other soon." And I says to him, "But they're very old, E. H." and E. H. says, according to his Mam, you're never too old.

Mrs W. she hasn't got a Mr W. like I haven't got a Dad, but Mr W. he died. He didn't go off to seek no fortune. And Mr Kendal, his Mrs Kendal ran off with the chimney sweep although my Gran says, "However she met the chimney sweep in all-electric flats, I'll never know."

Mrs Warren had put a big hem along the top of the curtains and Mr K. and E. H. threaded a strong bit of plastic rope through these hems, so that they'd pull backwards and forwards.

Then Mr Kendal and E. H. strung them up across the stage and after a bit, Mr Kendal said, "They'll do." I thought they were very exciting. Whizz, they went one way, and whizz, they went the other. We were all sat behind them and that's different to sitting in front of them. It's better.

Before we knew where we were, it was time for the concert. All the Mams and Dads and Grannies were pouring into the hall and everybody was sat down and Mr Kendal put up Stella Green's blackboard and easel at the side of the stage and he had a lot of big white cards with people's names written on them, like E. H. and the Dead Beats have.

Every time somebody went on, Mr Kendal was going to put one of these big white cards on the blackboard and easel.

Mr Jarvis said it was all a waste of time. He didn't think there were an eyeful there who could read anyway, and Mr Harris, he said if Mr Jarvis didn't "just shut up, if you don't mind", he, personally, would fling Mr Jarvis's chair through a window and Mr Jarvis straight after it.

I must say there's plenty of life round here.

Then, all of a sudden, there's this shout, "LIGHTS!" from Mr K., and Mrs Warren, who is standing near the door, she switches all the lights off and that threw everybody into a mad panic straight away, particularly Mavis Jarvis's Mam.

She screamed so loud I thought the hall would cave in. Mrs Warren goes, "What's wrong? What's wrong? Whatever's going on?" and Mr K. shouts, "Put the lights on, Mrs W." And she did and there was Mrs Jarvis with a great, big, fat spider on her knee.

She was just sat looking at it and her eyes are like their Mavis's, they stick out like anything. They looked as if they were on the

end of stalks this time and I half expected this spider to reach up with one of his legs and bop her one. But it didn't and it couldn't have been asleep because Mrs Jarvis was going, "Aaaagh! Aaaaagh!" and Mr Jarvis was sat looking at this spider gone out.

"Gerritoferme," Mavis's Mam yells and Mr Jarvis brings his fist down right on top of that poor old spider.

Crash, he goes, and this is Superman spider because instead of it going splat, and pegging out immediately, it jumps about three feet in the air and lands on Stella Green's Granny's head.

Mrs Green, she reaches up and gets it down in her hand and says, "Dratted kids. More trouble than they're worth," and she shoves this spider under Mavis's Mam's nose (who I thought was going to fall straight off her chair) and she says, "Rubber."

"Whaaat?" Mrs Jarvis squeaks and Mrs Green goes, "Rubber spider. It's not real. Did you think it was real?" and she starts laughing.

I thought Mavis's Mam was going to kill her, she looked so mad but by then her leg was hurting that much from where Mr Jarvis's fist had landed, she told him off instead.

"Stupid trick, that," Mr Kendal says. "Don't let it happen again," and Mavis J. smirks and walks away.

Mavis J. is really grotty.

Mr Kendal says, "Now, we're going to have to put the lights out to let the acts get on and off the stage. I hopes as you'll all bear with us," and everybody said they would, except Mrs Jarvis, she said the whole thing was barmy from beginning to end but nobody took a lot of notice so she shut up.

"Right," Mr Kendal says, and waves his hand at Mrs Warren and snap, off go the lights again and Mr K. falls over a chair and nearly breaks his neck.

"LIGHTS!" he screams and Mrs W. put them on again and Mr K. picked himself up, snarling at Mrs Jarvis who was laughing so much she was nearly choking, and then he waves to Mrs Warren and this time everything worked.

Mr Kendal flicked his torch on and found the first big white card and he put it on the blackboard and it said E. H. and the DEAD BEATS and then Mr K. yelled "LIGHTS!" Mrs W. switched them on and there, right in the middle of the stage, was E. H., Gary Smith and Stella Green's dog, Tiny, who was scratching himself and he wouldn't move not for anything. He just sat there and grinned at everybody from the middle of this snowstorm of dog hair which was flying all over the shop. It's a wonder that dog isn't bald but he never runs out of hair to scratch off.

It took three people to get Tiny off and then E. H. and the Dead Beats started playing. Well, they did very well. Everybody said, "Marvellous," and, "Great," and they clapped and clapped and clapped. So E. H. said, "We'll give you an encore then," and Mr Jarvis, he shouts, "That's what comes of encouraging them. They won't go home," and Mr Harris, he says, "Come down here and say that." Mr Kendal says, "Get on with it, then," to E. H., so E. H. starts to sing again and Gary (the Dead Beats), he starts banging his drum and then he gets carried away and dances round, his drumsticks flashing through the air like chopsticks.

As he's coming round the drums, E. H. steps back and Gary bangs straight into him. Old E. Harris, he goes flying onto his knees but he knows where it's at, does E. Harris. Quick as a flash, he bats Gary's legs with his fist, clasps his hands together and starts singing about how he wants his Mam.

"MAMEEE. MAAAAAMEEEE," he's going, and tells us all how far he'll walk just so his Mam'll smile at him, and from the middle of the hall, there comes this shout, "SON! SON!" and it's Mrs Harris, E. H.'s Mam. "HOLD ON, SON!" she shouts, and she's got half a tablecloth in her hand mopping her eyes with it because she's going sob, sob, "Oh, how touching," all the time, and she starts knocking everybody out of their seats to get to the stage and E. H. looks up, sees his Mam hurtling towards him, goes, "Aaaagh!" and dashes off and that was the end of that act.

Everybody said they enjoyed the encore better than the act. Mr Kendal said he'd have to put Mrs Harris on the stage next time and looked as if he'd just sucked a lemon.

Me and Mr Kendal pulled the curtains shut and Mrs Warren switched out the lights and then she put them on again and the white card said THE LADY FROM THE FISH AND CHIP SHOP.

I could see our Gran nodding her head and smiling but everybody else was going, "Oh. Cor blimey!" and moaning and groaning and there, in the middle of the stage, was the lady from the fish and chip shop and she had a big bowl of fish batter one side, and a big bowl of dead, wet fish on the other.

She didn't take any notice at all of the people sat in front of her. She just lifted her hand and after a bit everybody shut up, and then she said, "Ay am now going to attempt to break may own personal fish battering record." And she put about six hundred wet fish into this batter in about two seconds flat.

Well, you should have seen the front row. They were covered. Stella Green's Gran stood up and she says, "I don't know about fish being battered but if you flick another drop of that stuff on my coat, I'll batter YOU."

The fish and chip shop lady didn't seem to hear Granny Green. She just bowed and said, "Ay am happy to tell you, ay have beaten may own record by three wet fish." Mr Kendal started clapping and after a minute, everybody else clapped as well.

You should have seen that stage. We had to practically scrub it down before the next act but I'm happy to say we didn't get all the batter off because the next act was Mavis Jarvis.

When Mavis J. said she wanted to do a turn everybody thought Mr Kendal would drag in a couple of young palm trees, stick a coconut in her hand and tell her to get on with it, but he didn't. Why, I don't know.

He said, "Well, Mavis my girl, you're the only volunteer apart from E. H. and Gary," and he glared at us all. "What you gonna do?" he asks, and Mavis J. says, "It's a surprise."

Well, it were all of that. She gets on that stage and she's wearing nineteen bits of net curtain.

" 'Ere," Mr Kendal goes. "What are you doing?" but old Mavis J. was well into her stride by that time.

E. H. and the Dead Beats did the music and Mavis J. says, "I am now going to do the Dance of the Seven Veils which I was told about at school, because it is in the Bible, so everybody knows that's O.K. because if it's in the Bible then it has to be O.K." and Mr Jarvis is going, "Yers. Yers," and shouting, "great stuff. Bravo. Encore," and so far, the only thing Mavis has moved is her mouth.

So, anyway, E. H. and Gary do this music and then Mavis J. starts whipping these bits of curtain off and throwing them all over the shop.

Granny Green, who's still in the front row, she says, "My bright Christmas. If I'd 'a'known, I'd have sat outside," because she's draped head to foot in one of these bits of curtains.

Whip, whip, whip, off come the curtains until there's only one left and Mr Kendal says, "That'll do now, Mavis," but Mavis won't stop and she flings off this last bit of curtain and there she stands, in navy blue wool, down to her ankles and so far up her neck, she looks as if she's wearing ear muffs.

I must say it went down very well. Particularly when old Mavis took a bow and slipped on a bit of the fish and chip shop lady's batter. We all thought that was the best part.

Mr Kendal was going, "Come on, then. Get off, girl," but Mavis wouldn't move and when everybody got fed up of clapping, she said, "I can sing a song if you want," and started singing. But Mr Kendal wasn't going to have that and he shouted, "LIGHTS!" to Mrs Warren and him, E. H. and the entire band finally managed to get old Mavis J. off that stage.

By that time, we had to get through the rest of the acts in double quick time because if we hadn't, Mr K. said, "There'll be no time to march."

We all got lined up at the top of the hall and then Mr Kendal went, "Has everybody got their paper and combs?" and we had. "And have you got your tin plates, E. H. and Gary?" he goes on, and they had. "And has you got your sticks with the tennis balls on them?" he says, and we had. "Right," he shouts. "Instruments to mouths. GO!"

We marched very well down that hall. The only sticky bit came when we got to the bottom because Mr Kendal had forgot to put a bit of string on my hand and when he shouted, "RIGHT. *RIGHT*" I didn't know which way to go, so I ended up practically sharing Granny Green's chair, and everybody else ended up sitting with Mr Jarvis and three punk rockers, who started beating them off with the evening paper and two spare seat cushions.

Mr Kendal's still going "RIGHT, RIGHT, I say," and by the time me and Granny Green had got rid of each other (and that wasn't easy I can tell you, because she kept saying, "I've been in everything else, I might as well be in this too."), I was practically a nervous wreck, on account of how when I turned round, there was Granny Green right behind me, whistling through her fingers and making more noise than the rest of the band put together.

I wish I could whistle through my fingers.

I says to Mrs Green, "It's only for children this band," and she says, "Don't worry about that, Lily. Tonight's aged me, girl. I'm in my second childhood already."

Mrs Warren managed to get her to sit down again though, and me and the band met up in the middle of the hall and Mr Kendal was nowhere to be seen.

I didn't think very much of that, to tell you the truth, but after a couple of minutes I saw him and he was crouching down at the end of the back row of chairs.

"Come on, Mr Kendal," I shouts. "You

47

can't hide from us." And he lifted his head and he says, "Ain't that the truth," and then he leaps to his feet and marches at my side and when he shouts, "RIGHT," this time I follow him.

I thought I'd liven things up a bit, so that everybody could see what a good job Mr K. had done with the band, so I flung my stick in the air and I forgot all about Mr Kendal walking along with me, and when it came down, it went CRACK straight on the top of his head and he doesn't have a lot of hair, Mr K. Less than average.

I heard his teeth crunch.

He sort of staggered a bit and then he said, "Well done, Lily. The first fling of the night," and after that there was no stopping us. We all chucked our sticks up in the air and even Mavis J. didn't rattle Stella Green when Stella stuck her Union Jack up Mavis's nose.

"It was a mistake," their Karen said, and for once, old Poison Ivy didn't hit back.

Mr Kendal said it wasn't a bad sort of concert on the whole and we'd raised quite a bit of money.

"I don't think we'll do it again, though," he says. "There has to be easier ways than that of fund raising." But we're going to buy some kazoos, cymbals and half a drum with the money we've earned tonight.

"Instruments first. Uniforms next," Mr Kendal said.

That was the end of that night. I wonder what sort of uniforms we're going to have?

4

Formations?!

Mavis J. has been put on the drums because Mr K. managed to buy a sheepskin, and a big drum from another band that's closing down. The man who runs that band, he told Mr K. it was a bargain and a chance not to be missed so Mr K. took E. H. with him to try on this sheepskin, and E. H. put it on and Mr Kendal said he had to forcibly stop one of this man's kids from taking E. H. onto a bit of good grass.

"I'm telling you, if a butcher had seen him," Mr Kendal told Mrs W., "I wouldn't have answered for the consequences. Could have been served up with a bit of mint sauce come Sunday, that's all, drat it," and E. H. scowled and kicked Mavis J.

Of course, old Mavis bashed him back and Gary Smith, the Dead Beat, he had to pull them apart before Mr Kendal chucked them both out of the band for fighting, because that's what Mr Kendal says will happen to the very next people he finds fighting.

"We've no spirit of togetherness," he says. "And you can't build a band without a spirit of togetherness."

Personally, I'd as soon get together with a rattlesnake than Mavis J.

Anyway, Mr K. bought this sheepskin and drum because he said he had a feeling it might fit somebody else and when we turned up tonight, there he was with this pile of sheep beside him and he shouted, "Mavis. Come here, lass, and try this on," and Mavis J. she tried it on and it fitted.

"Put the drum on too, Mavis," Mr Kendal said because that was too big for E. H. to carry as well. When it was round his neck, he looked as if he was walking on his knees.

Old Mavis put this drum round her neck and she says, "This fits me smashing, Mr Kendal," and she goes off down the field banging and crashing on this drum like somebody not right.

"That'll do, Mavis," Mr K. said and he told her to take the drum off a minute while he adjusted it.

Just then, little Stella Green comes onto the field with her dog Tiny and I've never seen anything like what happened to Tiny. He must have seen old Mavis almost straight away because his head had no sooner got round the corner of the wall than he went stiff.

He stared at Mavis till I thought he would go cross-eyed and then he went whooof, and he was across that grass like a shot from a gun.

Mr Kendal, he looks up from this drum and he sees Tiny and he yells, "Mavis. Mavis. Tek that sheep off yer back, lass," but it was too late.

Tiny was herding old Mavis until she didn't know which way to move. If she went one way, he snapped at her ankles and if she went another, he banged her with his head.

51

He only wanted her to go one way and that was towards the way out. I think he was planning to take her home with him as a toy.

Old Mavis J. she starts running, which is just what Tiny wants and she's getting redder and redder but when she tries to stop, Tiny's right there at her heels, snapping and barking.

"Throw the sheepskin off," Mr Kendal's roaring and old M. J.'s screaming, "I can't. I can't." But then she manages to get it off somehow and she slings it as far away from her as she can.

"Rotten mongrel," she's calling Tiny and tries to kick him but Tiny's too quick for that. As soon as the sheepskin's gone, he sort of skids to a halt and looks up at Mavis as if to say, "There's always a next time," and then he just turns round and walks away.

Even when he walks past this pile of dead sheep on the ground, he only sniffs it.

" 'Cos it's not moving," E. H. says. "They only want them when they're moving."

I thought Mr Kendal would go mad. He stamps up to little Stella and he says to her, "Now then, Stella. Any more of that from your dog and you're out of the band. Can't have him chasing Mavis every time she puts that on. That's an important part of the band, that is." And Stella nods her head and says, "Sorry, Mr Kendal. If *It* had stood still, Tiny wouldn't have run her," but Mr Kendal wouldn't have any of that.

"Who's 'It' when she's at home?" he says. "You know what she's called, Stella, and if you want to be in the band, you'd better start calling Mavis her proper name." Then he looks at me and he says to Stella, "Now, what do you call her?"

Stella, she looks at me and then she says, "That's Piggylittle."

I says to her, "My name's Lily Pickle, Stella." And she says, "Yes, but everybody calls you Piggylittle."

Mr K. goes, "Oh well. Anyway, you keep that dog out of the way, else I'm warning you – no band."

Young Stella, she marches over to Tiny, who's nearly as big as their Karen and she gets hold of his great head and looks him straight in the eyes. Tiny starts licking her face but she says, "Tiny go home." And this dog's going slurp, slurp, and washing her to bits.

Then, Stella hits him right on the end of the nose and stamps her foot and says again, "Go home, naughty dog." And this poor old Tiny, he drops his head and starts slinking off across the field and we all stand and watch him till he gets to the opening.

"Poor old sausage," I say and E. H. says

sheepskins are only of any good to sheep, which they are, and if Mavis J. really had to dress up, then a goatskin would suit her a lot better.

"That'll do," Mr Kendal says.

"Complete with horns," says E. H. and gets a good telling off from Mr K. but he said it was worth it to see Mavis J's nasty face go purple.

Just as the last bit of Tiny's tail's going round the wall, a cat jumps up onto the gate and we all feel a lot better about the poor old dog then because he practically has this cat balancing on its toenails.

Spitttt! Hissssss! it's going, and turning round and round without its paws once touching solid ground.

Magic, they are, cats. No wonder they knock around with witches.

Mr Kendal, he shouts, "When you've all finished just standing there, perhaps you could get into line," and we go shuffle, shuffle, and get lined up.

"Tonight," Mr Kendal says, "I am going to try some formations." And everybody gulps and goes, "Formations. What's formations?"

"All you lot," Mr Kendal says, pointing to all the kazoo players, "you make two lines, kneeling down, facing each other." So they all kneel down practically with their noses touching.

"Good grief," Mr Kendal shouts, "leave a space between you. The band's got to march down there."

"Oh," they all go and make two more lines and this time they're so far apart, you need binoculars to see them.

"I don't know what I did to deserve this," Mr Kendal says and Mrs Warren, she says to Karen Green, "Now then, Karen. Come on and do it properly, there's a good girl." And poor old Karen is nearly sick on the spot, so she kneels down, then sits down and next time I look, she's flat on her back staring at the sky.

"Get up, Karen," Mr K's going, "get up." But old Karen, she says, "I don't think I want to be in the band any more, Mr Kendal." And Mr Kendal says, "Why not?" And Karen, she says, "I'm fed up of blowing on a bit of paper."

"Ah well, now then," Mr K. goes. "This is where we give you all a surprise." And he goes nod, nod, to Mrs Warren and she lifts up her shopping bag and opens it.

"Look," she says. "Kazoos, two tambourines and a triangle." And then she and Mr Kendal hand them all out.

Karen blows her kazoo, which is shaped

like a trumpet but sounds just the same as a piece of paper and a comb, and then she says, "Hmmmmm. Not bad, is it?" and when it comes to them making two lines and kneeling down again, she does it properly this time.

"Right, Lily," Mr K. says. "You lead your little lot down through the middle of the two lines. Have you got your string on your hand?" and I nods and behind me there's Michelle Parish and Samantha Collins holding up a big Union Jack, which is standing in for our Band flag till we get one, and then, behind each of them is a little lass, holding onto long white ribbons which are pinned onto the flag and then behind them, but walking in the middle is Stella Green. Behind her is Mavis Jarvis with her big drum and just at the back of her, Deirdre Summers with her triangle and then there's E. Harris and Gary Smith with their tin plates.

"Well," says Mr Kendal. "Just you look at that, Mrs W. Ain't that a sight for sore eyes?" And Mrs Warren says it is, it is.

"Now then, Lily," Mr K. shouts. "When I blow this whistle, I want you to start marching," and he blows the whistle and I start marching and I can hear these feet behind me going thud, thud on the grass.

We started marching down the middle of

them two lines and Mavis Jarvis was banging her big drum and it sounded smashing and then the drum stopped and all I could hear was this, "Ouch! Oooh!" and, "Gerroff!" and I turn round, and there's old Mavis, grinning all over her face, bashing all these kneeling kids on the head with her drumstick.

Bong, bong, bash, she's going but Mr Kendal, he isn't grinning and the next minute, he's got old Mavis walking on her toes on account of him helping her with the scruff of the neck and he's saying, "Naughty, Mavis. Not to do that," and then he lets her go when she promises she'll be good in future.

Karen Green's looking at her and she says, "You might think you've got away with it, Fatso, but you haven't."

"Get back in line," Mr Kendal shouts. "All of you, back where we started," so we go back to where we started and Mr Kendal says. "Any more trouble and there'll be no band. No band at all," and nobody says anything. Them kneeling down don't say anything because they're still recovering consciousness from where old M. J.'s bashed them and Karen Green, she just looks and looks with her eyes like little slits.

I must say I was glad it wasn't me she was

looking at but old Mavis, she wouldn't care if it was a tiger in front of her, it wouldn't bother her at all.

"Shall I go then?" I ask Mr Kendal and he shouts, "Yes. Right, now. When I blow the whistle, best feet forward." And he blows the whistle again and I start marching again and throw my stick in the air. Then I twirl it round a bit and Mavis J.'s still beating on her drum, bong, bong, bong, but then the sound changes and now all you can hear is this broing, scream, broing, yell, broing, "Maaaammmmmm!"

I stopped so fast that Michelle and Samantha had gone past me before they realised and I was smothered in the Union Jack. All I could see were red, white and blue stripes everywhere.

"Get me out of here," I start yelling, because Michelle Parish has dropped her end of the flag and now she's screaming, "Look what Mavis Jarvis is doing to Stella Green." And it takes me about sixteen hours to get out of that flag so that I can see for myself.

I can't hardly believe it when I do see it. There's Mavis J. standing there banging on her drum and inside it is Stella Green.

"How did she get in there?" I says to E. H. because by that time we're all back across that field and dragging Stella out of the way.

She comes out and tries to stand up but she can't and she goes flop on the ground.

I says to Mavis, "You rotten bully. Here, take that," and I bash her straight in the chest and Mavis goes push with her drum and sends me flying.

E. H. picks his finger nails and says, "Better watch out, their Karen is coming," and there's Karen coming up that field as if she's a human cannonball fresh from a cannon.

Old M. Jarvis, she just stands there sneering, but she sneers on the other side of her face when Karen gets to her.

Whoosh, Karen goes and the drum flies up in the air and then we see it hasn't got no bottom.

"Dropped it over Stella's head, didn't she?" E. H. says, polishing his teeth with a burnt out match. E. H. never fights with girls. He says it's beneath him. "Whoever heard of a lad belting a lass?" he says and I tell him, plenty of people have heard of it. Three quarters of the lads round here look on beating up lasses as part of their life's work.

E. H. says no pop star would ever do that.

"Spoil my hands for a start," he says. But I think it's because the lass here is Mavis J. who is three times bigger than E. H. and Gary Smith put together.

I don't say anything, though, because I wouldn't want to see Mavis J. beat E. Harris. If she did that, I'd probably have to buy an old football from the junk shop and fit it onto her head.

I like E. H.

By now, though, Karen has got this drum off Mavis and she's yelling, "I'll kill yer. I'll massacre yer," (this writing business isn't easy. I had to go down to the Library and look 'massacre' up in the dictionary) and Mavis is yelling, "Yeah. You and whose army?" and Karen says, "An army of one – me!" and flattens her.

'Course, old M. J. can't hardly move then because she's buried in sheepskin and her legs are as thick as tree trunks so between them, they keep her on the ground longer than she should have been because up comes old Tiny again.

"Loves sheep, that dog, don't he?" says E. H. and Mr Kendal's going, "No wonder it's a bargain, dratted thing. I don't reckon it's been cured properly." And if cured means stopping it smelling, well it hasn't, because this sheepskin is smelling like mad.

Tiny likes it though. He gets a great mouthful of it, lifts up his head, looks all thoughtful and then starts trotting off back across the field.

That doesn't work too well because he sort of goes erk, only in a doggy voice, like a woof and an erk together, and his head nearly gets pulled away from his body because old Mavis J. is still on the other end of this sheepskin and you can tell Tiny forgot that there for a minute or two.

It doesn't stop him though. He just gets a better grip and whips his bottom round the other way and starts pulling. He has old Mavis moving across that grass at a good rate before we know where we are.

"Gerroff," she's shouting. "Get this dog off'er me." And Mr Kendal looks at Tiny pulling his lead drummer and her sheepskin across the field and he says, "I don't believe it."

"Gerrit off me," yells old Mavis J. Nobody can move at all now for laughing and Karen Green is beating the grass with her fists, she's that happy.

Anyway, Mr Kendal suddenly dashes across to Mavis J. and grabs her ankles and what with Tiny on one end and Mr K. on the other, I reckon M. J. grew three inches in three seconds there.

Then, little Stella sits up, who has been forgotten about all together, and she starts shouting, "Kill It, Tiny. Kill It." And Mrs Warren goes, "Be quiet, Stella." But Stella keeps shouting and every time she shouts, Tiny gets a better grip on the mouthful of sheepskin he's got already.

It had to end, though, and Mr Kendal made Tiny let go and he dragged Mavis J. to her feet and he says, "You ought to be ashamed of yourself, my girl. You could have deafened that little lass." And Mavis goes, "It were an accident. Honest, it were an accident. She stopped walking and next thing I knew, she were inside me drum."

Mr Kendal goes, "What? Are you sure?" And Mavis J. says, "Yes, I'm sure."

"Did anybody see what happened?" Mr Kendal shouts and everybody looks at everybody else and then Mr Kendal says to Deirdre Summers, "Did you see what happened, Deirdre? You were right behind them." And Deirdre shakes her head and says, "I was playing on my triangle. It's not easy to play, you know."

Mr Kendal goes, "Right. Right." Then he turns to E. H. and the Dead Beat and he says, "Did either of you two see anything?" And they both shake their heads and say, "Not a thing."

Mr Kendal thinks a minute and then he says to Stella, "Did you stop?" And she nods, "But I didn't stop long," she goes. "And this drum fell over my head."

Mr Kendal says we'll have to take Mavis's word for it, "in view of the fact that there's no proof to the contrary," and he says to Mavis J., "Well, Mavis my girl, I'm sorry if we've misjudged you." Then he thinks a bit and says, "Take that sheepskin off. I'm going to have it cleaned properly. That dratted dog'll never keep away otherwise."

All I know is we all clubbed together and bought old Tiny the next biggest bone we could get. The biggest would have been Mavis J. but she wouldn't lie down.

I hope the next time I write, the words get easier. I'm practically living at that Library these days and I can tell you, I never see anybody there I know and is it to be wondered at.

Last time I went, three plastic roof tiles fell off and landed at my feet and the Librarian goes, "Did you do that?" and I says, "No." And she looks up at this ceiling one hundred feet above my head and she smiles and says, "Of course you didn't. Have a sweet?"

What a life.

5

Bang, bang, you're dead, Kojak

I never thought I'd ever write nice things about old Mavis Jarvis but here I am, almost writing them.

We had a lot of trouble at the band practice on Wednesday night because when we got there, these kids called The Red Hand Band of Rat-Trap Flats were waiting for us, but this isn't the same sort of band as the Workton Whistlers, you bet your life it isn't.

This band, the Red Hand band, they only cause trouble and beat people up as soon as look at them. Once, they busted all E. H. and the Dead Beat's drums and guitar up. E. H. said, "We tried to stop them but there were eight of them and only me and Gary." So they didn't get very far.

When we got to the field, they were all lined up on the wall. Not sitting on the wall, standing. They were miles above us and they started spitting and kicking when we went past.

Peggy Lane was stood at the very end and when I got to her, I looked up at her and I said, "You spit at me, Peggy Lane, and I'll be up there with you." And she sort of sneered and went, "Coo, 'ark at 'er. Oo do you think you are, then? Lady Muck?"

Karen Green grabbed my arm and she says, "Come on. Ignore them. They're not worth bothering about." Just then Mr Kendal came up the road.

"'Ere," he roars. "You lot get off that there wall and take your hooks home."

"Oo's gonna make us?" they all shouted, so Mr Kendal, he shoved us all through the gate, which is twisty because there's a hole in the wall and right in front of you, there's a fence. You have to walk to the end of this little fence and then turn right and you're into the field. Nobody ever does that, though, they all climb the fence and jump over. Thing is, you can get caught in that space if somebody wants to get you and then you've got a job and a half getting away.

Mr Kendal looks at this gate and he says, "When you go out, if you go out on your own, don't use the gate. Jump over the wall." I says to E. H., "He knows a thing or two, Mr Kendal." And E. H. says, "That's what comes of being in the army and being Ever Ready."

I don't know about that but Mr Kendal does the best imitation of Stan Laurel I have ever seen in my life. He stands there and he's very thin like S. Laurel was and he twists his hair round and he even talks like him.

I can do a Kojak. I stick a lollipop in my mouth and go, "Who loves ya, baby?" but nobody ever seems to know who it is I'm doing – only my Gran, she knows. She always says, "Yes, that's a really good Kojak but perhaps you've a little bit too much hair?" and she laughs.

I bet if I were bald, everybody would know it was Kojak straight away. "Who loves ya, baby?" bang bang, you're dead. That's Kojak.

Peggy Lane doesn't have to bother at all. All she has to do to look like somebody else is stand on tiptoe and then she looks exactly like our Christmas Tree Fairy. My Granny says she can't believe how bad Peggy Lane is because she looks so good. She has gold hair, not even yellow like some people. Hers is gold and it's long and she wears it straight with a parting in the middle, and she's got blue eyes and little red lips and pink cheeks, and she makes everybody else's cheeks pink as well when she's around because she swears like a trooper.

All the swear words I know, I learnt off Peggy Lane, but she wasn't too bad till she started going round with this Red Hand lot. Then she got terrible.

She hasn't got gold hair now, she's got half of it pink, half of it purple and half of it gone. She's got it that short, it looks as if somebody's cut it with a broken bottle. All jagged, with three green spikes on the front.

She wears a tartan kilt that hangs right down to her ankles and on her feet she has big black winter boots with yellow wool socks inside them. She wears her Dad's pyjama top underneath her boy friend's black leather motor bike jacket, which is only about six sizes too big for her and on the back of that, she has these words painted: 'AWFUL WARNING' and they're painted in red paint which has run and it looks just like blood.

I must say it suits her. She's always going, "I'm warning you," and then telling you what she's going to do to you.

"I'm going to make you into two dozen tins of dog food" she goes.

Karen Green says, "She's very honest, that Peggy Lane. She's the most awful person I've ever known," and then she thinks a bit and says, "Except for Mavis Jarvis, that is," and we all think about this and then we nod.

Peggy Lane can't turn you into a tin of dog food but Mavis Jarvis can.

So, this Wednesday night, Awful Warning and her lot all stand watching us practise and Mr Kendal tells them to get out of it and they won't. Then, Peggy Lane picks up a stone and she throws it at Stella Green, who is about two feet tall and not hurting anybody.

Me and their Karen, we're over at that wall like a shot and it was very scary, I can tell you, because no sooner were we there than Awful Warning shouts, "Down," and all her gang jump down and get round us.

"What do you want?" Peggy says and that sounds as if she's got a mouthful of razor blades.

"You leave young Stella alone," I tells her. And Karen says, "If that stone had hit her, you'd be counting teeth now."

Awful Warning suddenly shoots a hand out and cracks Karen straight across the face and I see she's got big thick heavy rings on her fingers and they've got jewels sticking out of them.

When I look at Karen's face, it's spurting blood all over because these rings have cut into her face.

I think hmmmm, so I kick A. W. as hard as I can and duck at the same time. That must have been the best thing I ever did as well because old Peggy, she whips her hand up without even thinking about it and it goes zoom, smack, straight into one of her pal's faces. That didn't go down very well, I can tell you, but that's when the fun started.

Mr Kendal, he started shouting, "Oy, you leave them lasses alone," and he comes charging over that field towards us but Peggy, she's got a safety pin hanging from one ear and she's not bothered about no Mr Kendal. She just starts stomping on me while her mates grab Karen.

I thought my last hour had come because not only did Awful Warning start kicking me, but three quarters of her gang did as well. I reached up and clawed four long paths right down P. L.'s leg because one thing I don't like is people kicking me. Miss Frankenstein goes, "Aaaagh!" and lifts her leg up to have a better look.

That's when I pushed her as hard as I could and that's when somebody kicked me in the face. I could feel all my teeth loosen in my head. I thought if I stood up, they'd drop out, so I kept my face down.

Karen Green, she was kicking out like wildfire but she couldn't use her hands because this gang, they had them pulled behind her. It was all happening in about half a minute because I knew Mr Kendal was coming, running and it was happening while he was running towards us.

Then, there came this great roar, Rrrraa-aggghhhhh! it went. Everybody went like Pinocchio, stiff as boards, because all the blood in people's bodies had gone zonk when it screeched to a halt and stopped running and turned into instant ice. Then we all turned our heads real slow and there was Mavis J. the Orang-outang coming round that gate like Flash Gordon and the Avenging Angel put together.

"Lerremgo," she kept on shouting. "Lerremgo." And Awful Warning, she screamed, "Let them go. Let them go." And then she takes off down that field like a shot from a gun but she didn't get far, because old Mavis J., she was right in there and she'd got hold of Peggy and was twisting her arm round her back in next to no time.

"Come on," she says. "You're coming with me," and she brought P. L. back up the field. "Say you're sorry to Piccalilli," Mavis goes and Peggy Lane looks at me and spits as hard as she can.

Mavis Jarvis bounces her up and down then. "Say you're sorry," she says, and A. Warning, whose eyes have practically forgotten to come down with her face from the bouncing, she goes, "Sorry."

"Sorry, Lily," Mavis says and Peggy sort of snarls and then says, "Sorry, Lily," and then old M. J., she frog marches her to the wall and says to her mates, who are really great pals they are, all stood in a line behind the wall with Karen Green between them, Mavis J. says, "Let Karen go," and they do, without any arguing, and then Mavis sort of chucks Awful Warning over the wall back to her pals.

"Don't come round here causing trouble again," Mavis Jarvis says and I wouldn't have been surprised if fire hadn't come down her nose, she was that mad.

Peggy Lane stood there with her pink and purple hair and she shouts, "We'll get you. You see if we don't," and then they all go off and they don't hurry either. They go slouch, slouch, kick, down that road and P. Lane keeps looking back towards the field and I can't help but see she's looking at me particularly.

I says to Mavis J. "Thanks very much, Mavis," and Karen, she says, "Thank you, Mavis." And Stella Green, she comes up and says, "Kill It," to her dog Tiny, but Karen rattles her and tells her M. J. is O.K. O.K.? And she's not to call her 'It' any more and she's not to tell their Tiny to kill either.

Stella thinks about this for a minute but she won't say she's sorry like she's been told to, so Mavis Jarvis shouts, "Rotten little kid.

I'll put you under my drum again if you don't say you're sorry." And Karen Green goes, "Did you put her under that drum on purpose then?"

Mavis J. goes "Ha, ha, ha. 'Course I did," and that's the end of anything nice about old Poison Ivy.

Next minute, she's trying to shove our teeth down our throats, as usual, and mine felt as if she wouldn't have to shove very much.

Mr Kendal shouts, "I've never seen anything like it. Come on, leave each other alone and let's get on with this band practice."

The first time I throw my stick up in the air, I catch my hand on my mouth and one of my teeth falls straight out.

"It's not a front one, is it, E. H.?" I shout and E. H. says, "Smile." I think, smile, when I'm stood there with half of my face practically missing and three quarters of my teeth falling out of my head. But E. Harris, what does he care, he just says, "Go on, smile, if you want me to tell you." So I open my mouth and smile.

E. Harris goes, "Aaaaagh!" and puts a hand over his eyes. "Mein Gutness," he shouts. "Vot is dis? Can dis be Dracula's daughter?" and then he peers at me through his fingers and goes, "It can."

Why does everybody practise being funny on me, that's what I want to know.

In the end, Karen Green says, "It's not a front tooth, Lily. You're all right."

Mrs Warren says, "You'll have to put it under your pillow, Lily, for the Tooth Fairy," and laughs.

I just look at her. She must think I'm about three. The last time I put a tooth under my pillow for the Tooth Fairy, my Mam came and put a ten penny piece there and then my Dad came and borrowed it.

"I'll give it you back," he said and he never. He took it with him when he went to seek his fortune.

When I told my Gran, she said, "Most people's fortunes are other people's pennies, Lily." Then she sighed and went on, "I daresay he'll bring it back one day." But he hasn't. Not yet he hasn't.

Mr Kendal shouts, "Come on, then. We've got time for one more march before we call it a night." We line up again and Mr Kendal blows his whistle and we start marching and I sees this row of heads bobbing up and down behind the wall.

I looks at them and thinks, "That's queer," and throws my stick up in the air and just as I was going to catch it, splat, this runny squashy thing landed straight in my face.

The next second, there were hundreds of them flying through the air towards us. I could hear Mr Kendal shouting, "What the heck?" but I couldn't see anything on account of my eyes being full of blood.

"I'm bleeding," I starts screaming and old E. H.'s voice says, "It's tomato, you dope," and I wipe my eyes on my sleeve and then I see Peggy Lane and her Red Hand Gang tearing round us throwing mushy tomatoes out of brown paper bags. They were six pence a pound in the market, frying tomatoes, and I bet the stall people dumped them and then Awful Warning and her pals fetched them to throw at us.

We were all covered in tomato. You've never seen anything like it. Old Mavis J., her lovely sheepskin that she's so proud of, it looked as if the sheep was still in it.

Drums and kazoos and triangles went everywhere and we ran that gang out of the field but what a mess we all looked.

"What am I going to tell my Mam this time?" Karen Green wails. "Look at our Stella, smothered in tomato pips. Last time, she was covered in mud and tadpoles."

Mrs Warren sighed and said, "I'll take her home, Karen." And Karen, she shoved their Stella at Mrs Warren so fast, if Stella had been a match, she'd have caught fire.

Mavis J. is trying to talk but she can't. I thought she was mad before but that's nothing compared to now.

"I'll kill her," she says at last but, before she had a chance, something happened to Peggy Lane.

She got caught raiding the fruit shop the very next morning and the bobbies went to her Mam and Dad's, and her Mam and Dad, they made her wash all the pink and purple out of her hair and wipe off her lipstick. She had to unglue her false eyelashes and take her safety pin out of her ear, so that her Dad could clout her one across it, he said, put on a skirt and jumper and then they made her go to school in the afternoon.

That caused a commotion, I can tell you. E. H. said the teacher looked at her when she walked in, on account of her being in E. H.'s class and he said she went, "Who are you?" It was so long since they'd seen her.

"This is Elizabeth Lane," her Dad said, "and she's come to school and to school she stays."

Miss Cropper, the teacher, she said, "Sit down, Elizabeth Lane." And Awful Warning sat down with her faded hair and her clean face and her pink lips and answered some questions and stuck the end of her biro into Deirdre Summers's leg.

Deirdre went scream, and Miss Cropper said, "That girl there. The one making that disgusting noise," and Deirdre looked all round the class, pointed at herself and went, "Me, Miss?" and Miss Cropper snarled, "Yes, you, Miss," and has Deirdre out in front.

"What happened?" Miss Cropper asked, but E. H. said before old D. S. could tell her, Peggy Lane flicked some old mashed up chewing gum at Deirdre which missed her and landed on Miss Cropper's white blouse and there it stuck.

"Weren't white then," E. H. went.

The upshot of it all was that A. Warning got kept in and her Dad went mad and said she had to join the band with Mr Kendal.

"You *will* learn to behave, my girl," her Dad said. "And Mr Kendal's the one to teach you. He was in the army, was Mr K. He'll size you up right." And he marched her to the field that very night, which happened to be Thursday.

I thought Mavis J. was going to explode when she saw her but she didn't. She didn't say nothing at all, just told Mr K. she had to go home a minute.

"Well, don't be long," Mr K. says. "Band's not the same without the big drum." Mavis J. said she wouldn't be hardly five minutes and she just stood a bit and stared at Peggy Lane.

Awful Warning stuck her tongue out at her and we all waited for M. Jarvis to tear it from P. Lane's head but she didn't do nothing.

"She must be scared of her," Karen Green said, but I said, "Mavis Jarvis ain't scared of nothing." But then, neither is A. Warning, so we did wonder what was going to happen.

We soon found out.

Mavis Jarvis came back to the field and stood there putting her sheepskin on and then her drum and then, when she's all ready, she walks up to Peggy Lane and she says, "This is what you done." And she points to all these sticky tomato stains which Mr K. couldn't get out straight away.

"They'll have to wear off, Mavis," he'd said.

After Mavis Jarvis had said that, Awful Warning goes sneer, sneer, "So what?" and the next minute, M. J. whips her hand up from behind her drum and she's got a gun.

Mr Kendal turns round just then and he sees this gun and he shouts, "Mavis. Put that down, girl," and his voice makes all goose pimples come on my skin.

I know a gun when I see one. They're always shooting each other on telly but here's old Mavis, standing with a gun in her hand and then she goes, "You'll not throw any more tomatoes," and she looks that wild, even Peggy Lane's scared to death.

Mavis J. shouts, "You dirty rat," (Like James Cagney, you know) and then she shoots her!

BANG! this gun goes and it's so loud, it nearly deafens you. Peggy Lane seems to rise three feet off the ground without twitching a finger. Honest, if she could do that normally, she'd be made for life. People'd pay thousands to see her.

Anyway, she goes up in the air and then sort of goes smack flat backwards, without even bending in the middle a little bit. Just smack flat backwards and E. H. said that if he could do that when he was rock and rolling, he'd clear the floor.

Peggy Lane lies on the grass, flat out, just as if she'd been ironed and she'd got one hand clutching her chest where her heart would be, if she had one, that is.

"Aaaagh!" she sort of croaks. "She got me!" and Mr K., his face is as white as a sheet.

"What you done, girl?" he says, and his voice is shaking like a leaf. "What you done?" and Mavis J. starts laughing, and she laughs so much she crumples up in a heap on the ground leaning over her big drum which is still strapped to her back.

Mr Kendal looks at her for only a second and then he's at Awful Warning's side and he's knelt down and he's saying, "Where does it hurt, Peggy? Where does it hurt, gal?" and Peggy L. she looks up and tears are spurting out of her eyes like water out of fountains and she says, "In my chest."

Mr K. says, "Now look, Peggy. I just want you to move your hand so I can see how bad it is," and we're all standing there, frozen to the spot.

You could have heard a pin drop, you could, even if you'd dropped it on that grass, it was so quiet.

Peggy Lane moves her hand and Mr Kendal peers down at this chest and he says, "Where is it, Peggy?" and Peggy L. goes, "Where's what?" and she doesn't sound very happy. Mind you, if I'd just been shot, I don't suppose I'd sound happy either.

"The gun shot wound," Mr K. says and Peg lifts her head up, looks down at her chest and goes, "I must have the wrong side." So then she looks at the other side of her chest but there's nothing there either.

"Well, it's here somewhere," old Peg goes and jumps up onto her feet and starts looking for this hole in her skin.

Mr Kendal's still knelt down and he looks up at Elizabeth Lane dancing around, and he says, "Are you sure you've been shot?" and Awful Warning says, "Well, you saw it. You heard it," and Mr K. nods.

He did, so he has to nod.

By this time, Mavis J. is purple with laughing and when she's got strength, she lifts her left hand up and waves it about.

"Is this what you're looking for?" she says, and collapses over her drum again. She's practically sobbing with laughter.

Mr Kendal goes snarl, leaps to his feet and

rushes over and drags this thing out of old M. J.'s hand and it turns out to be all what's left of a giant sized balloon that Mavis J. stuffed up her drum and stuck with a pin, at the same time as she pulled the trigger on her brother's toy gun.

Mr K. nearly went spare.

"It's a wonder I haven't gone white," he roars, and tries to haul M. J. to her feet but he can't. Not with the drum and the sheepskin as well.

Peggy Lane seethed when she saw she'd been tricked but you can't teach folk like that a lesson. I only said to her, "If you could do that jumping in the air and falling flat on your back routine again, Peggy, you could go on the stage with it." And she clonked me one.

Mr Kendal just turned round, lifted his finger and said, "There'll be no more fighting." And we both stopped.

I don't think A. Warning really had the heart for it.

Well, we all went home then. Old Mavis J. was still draped over her drum chortling her stupid head off the last time I saw her. They reckon she didn't stop laughing till midnight.

Nobody else seemed to find it very funny except Karen Green with her cut cheek and little Stella. They laughed like drains. I think it was that gun that did it for the rest of us. It didn't seem very funny when we saw old Mavis aiming that there gun at Peggy Lane.

Oh well, uniforms next week. We've been measured for them and Mrs Warren's got somebody to make them. Karen Green's Granny.

My Mam said, "Well, I only hope they turn out better than those hankies she made."

"Hankies?" I says, thinking what can you do wrong with hankies. My Mam said, "You may well ask. Have you ever seen round hankies before?" So now I'm wondering what we're all going to look like.

One thing, we have to look better than we do in our wellies.

6

The short skirt scandal

We went to try our uniforms on and half of them were made by Granny Green and half of them by Karen's Mam.

Karen and Stella's uniforms were made by

their Mam but mine and Mavis J.'s were made by their Granny and you could tell.

We went into the Old People's Hall and Mrs Green came in with her half of the uniforms and everybody was putting them on and saying, "My, they're lovely, these uniforms are," and, "Look at me. I look better than you do," and even, "Do you think red really suits me?" That was Michelle Parish, who has hair so red, if she stands still, everybody says, "Who left that traffic light there?"

Michelle goes, "Green's my colour – or blue. Blinking red. You can't tell where I start and where I finish," but she was a lot luckier than we were.

Granny Green was late coming for a start and when she did come, she sort of sidled in and put these two big suitcases down on the floor and then she sat down. Mrs Warren says, "Oh, Mrs Green. I'm glad you've come. We were just getting worried about you," and she laughed, ha ha.

Granny Green goes, "Yes, well, I was very busy," and then Mrs Warren says, "Well, shall we . . . erm, you know, shall we get on?"

Granny Green tippled the suitcases onto the floor and snapped the locks back on one and then takes out this pile of clothes. They looked lovely. There were jackets with thick gold braiding on them, and a cape for one of the little girls who was going to hold the banner. There was everything you could think of.

We had a very good time trying it all on until we got to the skirts. The other half of the band were parading up and down and swinging round in their little pleated skirts which came about one inch below their bottoms. Mrs Warren says to Granny Green, "Where are the skirts?" and Granny Green unlocked the other suitcase and she says, "Here," and hands one of these skirts to Mrs Warren.

Mrs Warren holds this skirt up and goes, "Hmmmmmmm." And then she says, "It . . . er, it isn't a bit on the long side, is it, Mrs Green?" And we all stand looking at this bale of cloth that's trying to be a skirt. It was so long that even held up in the air, its hem touched the floor.

I says, "Whose is that?" and looks round for this giant Granny Green must have measured.

Granny Green says, "It's yours, lass. It'll fit you a treat." By this time all Mrs Green's uniforms are standing round us, laughing their heads off, they are.

Mrs Warren looks at Granny Green and

then she says to me, "Try it on, dear." So I went round the back of the curtain and tried it on and when I came out, I says, "All I need is a bunch of flowers and a bride and I'm all set." Because, honest, it was just as long as a bridesmaid's frock.

Mrs Warren sighs and then says to Granny Green, "They're all too long, aren't they?" and starts pulling one skirt after another out of the suitcase.

Granny Green goes, "All depends on what you mean by long."

Mrs Warren says, "There's not a lot of other things I could mean by long. They're too long. Look at them. How are they going to march in skirts like that?"

Granny Green says, "I don't hold with young girls going round half naked."

That made us jump, I can tell you.

Mavis Jarvis comes up and she says, "Where's mine?" to Granny Green and Granny Green hands it to her and old M. J. she goes behind the curtain to try it on and when she came out, it was just as if one of those barrage balloons had landed.

She sort of flowed when she walked and her skirt billowed out all round her.

"I like this," she said. "I want my skirt long."

Mrs Warren says, "Don't be so silly. Go

and take it off," and Mavis J. said well, she agreed with Granny Green. Nobody should be allowed to walk around half naked and then Mrs W. lost her temper and told M. Jarvis if she didn't take the skirt off immediately, if not pronto, then she would have trousers made for her and there would be no skirt at all.

Old Mavis, she looked at Mrs Warren and then she says, "Trousers are a good idea. Why can't I have trousers?"

Mrs Warren goes, "Instead of a pretty little skirt?" and M. Jarvis, she goes cross-eyed and says, "I don't like pretty little skirts." And I must say, she's got a point.

Last time she played netball at school in her school shorts, the other team mistook her legs for two extra players and tried to have the game called off. They lost 43-1.

Mrs Warren goes, "Well, if that's what you want, Mavis, then we'll have to see what can be done."

When Mrs Green came up to have a look at the skirts, Mrs Warren says to her, "I'm afraid all these will have to be made again, Mrs Green. Your Mother doesn't seem to want to do them, so I wondered if you would."

Mrs Green said she would and patted her Mam on top of the head.

"Never mind, Mam," she said. "They'll be wearing stockings." But Granny Green just muttered and went off.

The uniforms weren't ready for another week but, by the time we got them, Mr Kendal had told us we were going to march in a Band Playing Contest the next Sunday.

We nearly all fainted with shock because this contest, it meant all the bands had to march through the streets in the town.

"What about our sticks?" I says to Mr K. "We can't hardly march with my Mam's old brush handle and a tennis ball." Mr Kendal said, "No, you can't," and looked all thoughtful. "Nearly forgot about them," he says. Then he goes, "Well, we haven't got the money to buy maces yet, so I think we'll probably have to cancel Sunday."

Everybody went, oh, moan, groan, and then E. Harris, he says, "What if I can make them there brush handles look like maces, Mr K?" and Mr K. says, "And how will you do that, Elvis?"

"Just call me The King," E. Harris says. And Mr Kendal says, "Would you like me to bow as well?"

"Only if you want to," E. H. tells him.

Mr Kendal goes bright red, which is never a very good sign with grown-ups. Going bright red means one of two things with them. Either they're going to drop dead at your feet or they're going to start shouting at you. Either case, you're a lot better out of the way.

E. H. looks at old Mr K. and he goes, "Just joking, Mr Kendal, just joking." And then Mr Kendal says, "Well, how're you going to get them to look like the real thing?"

"You just leave it to me," E. H. says, and I think how clever he is. It's not everybody who would think to sew sequins onto a bootlace and then wear it as a tie, but E. H. did.

I don't think there's anything E. Harris can't do, except for dancing, that is. He can't dance.

Last time he went on a dance floor, there were about six thousand kids on it with him. In two seconds flat, he'd cleared them all off.

"This is a dance I invented called The Windmill," he says to me, and then he started. His arms went round as if he were trying to fly. Well, he never got off the ground but twenty-three kids around him did. Sock, sock, sock, his fists went and he didn't even know he'd hit them.

After that, he flung himself forward on to the floor and, at the very last second, dropped his arms down so that his teeth didn't end up in all that wood. He didn't give any warning he was going to do this. He just went down as if he'd been felled. Crash, the floor went, and at the same time he went "Ahhh. Ahhhh. Ahhhh." I thought he'd broken both his wrists but he hadn't. That was just part of his Windmill dance as well.

"Come on," he says. "Come and do it with me."

E. Harris is very long when he's standing up, but when he's lying on the floor with his arms in front of him, he's longer still. I didn't want to spend all night running round him so I wouldn't go and dance with him.

Just as well, because when he got up and went into the next bit of his dance, he says, "This is The Hitch-hiker," and starts jerking his thumb backwards and forwards and the next thing that happened, Mr Johnson, who runs the Club, he's giving old E. H. a lift with E. H.'s left ear.

"Out," he shouts. "Out and stay out. Look at these 'ere kids," and E. H. looks and it's like a hospital in there. Bumps and bruises all over the place.

I says to Mr Johnson, "It's a new dance, Mr Johnson." And Mr J. says, "He doesn't need a dance floor. He needs a football field." So E. Harris and his sequin bootlace were chucked out into the street and I had to go with him, me and Gary the Dead Beat.

My Gran says, "Is he your boy friend then? Elvis Harris?"

I says to her, "He's not my boy friend, Gran, because I don't believe in boy friends," and my Gran says, "Why not?"

I says to her, "I don't want no boy friend who's going off to seek his fortune like my Dad did."

My Gran says, "They don't all go off to seek their fortune, gal. Some of them stay at home and go to work."

I told my Gran that E. Harris was not one of those.

"E. Harris," I told her. "He's going to London to make his fortune as a pop star and, when he's rich and famous, then he's going to send for me to dance for him in front of his band."

"And will you go?" she says, and I tell her I will not go because I shall be busy in London myself making my own fame and fortune.

"That way," I says. "Nobody gets to go and leave me."

My Gran nods and says, "Very right too."

I expect I shall still lend E. Harris my Jungle Juice hand cream which he rubs into his hair to drive all the girls wild, he says.

I haven't seen anybody get close up to E. Harris and go wild yet. Mostly they get close, have a sniff and reel into the nearest chair, but you can't tell E. H. anything. I wouldn't expect to, though. Not somebody called Elvis.

Anyway, what E. H. does with these brush handles, he takes them home and brings them to the band last thing on Sunday morning, and they're really beautiful.

They're all long and black and shiny and he's made these silver tops for them by wrapping up the tennis balls in his Mam's silver cooking foil and sellotaping them to the brush handles.

"Safe as houses," he tells Mr K. "They'll never come off, no matter what."

Mr K. looks at these maces and then he says to E. Harris, "I've underestimated you, lad. I reckon I owe you an apology." And he clapped his hand on E. H.'s shoulder.

It was just like one of those old films they put on telly where everybody starts looking all brave and they practically gnaw their lips to bits. It's almost always two blokes who've been sentenced to be shot or something and everybody knows they're going to get saved anyway.

Still, E. H. and Mr Kendal must have seen the same films as me because they knew how to do it. E. Harris shot up five inches taller and tried to look *trustworthy* and all that, and Mr Kendal stared bravely at the dog food factory chimney till I thought his eyes wouldn't ever be able to see anything else again.

After a bit though, they'd both had enough and old E. Harris shrank back down and Mr Kendal started roaring at us all to get into line.

"Fall in," he's yelling. "Fall in." And then all the equipment's put in this bus, which has been hired for the afternoon from Chambers' Vehicle Hire which is at the bottom of the flats, round the corner.

This bus must be about one hundred years old because it's practically held together with string and it's a double decker as well.

Mrs Warren shouts, "Now, has everybody got their gloves?" and we all wave our white gloves in the air. "And your jackets, and your skirts, your shoes and your white socks? Your hats and your capes?" And we all had everything and so the bus started.

When we gets to where the bands are going to start from, Mrs Warren put all old sheets up at the bus windows downstairs and we got changed.

Mavis Jarvis needed so much room, Stella Green and three other little kids had to stand on the seats and change.

Stella Green managed to get her jacket on back to front and their Karen went spare.

"Dumb kid," she snarls and yanks this jacket off Stella and grabs her arm and stuffs it down a sleeve. When she tried to stuff the other arm into the other sleeve, I thought she was going to break it in two to make it fit.

Their Stella's going, "Waaaah, I wanna go home." And Mrs Warren's going, "There, there, Stella. Don't cry," and then she tells Karen off. By the time Stella's got dressed, she's lost her hat.

"Where is it?" Karen shouts, staring at Stella as if she could murder her. "Where's your hat?" and then she looks round and sees this hat and she picks it up, says, "Here it is," slams it on Stella's head and goes away.

Poor old Stella is stood there on the bus seat as blind as a bat. Can't see a thing because Karen's put Mavis J's hat on Stella's head and

Mavis J. is trying to force Stella's hat on her head.

"Here's your hat," I says to Mavis because she's just getting ready to rip Stella's hat straight down the seams, and I take the hat off Stella's head and Stella's eyes are as big as buckets.

"Dark in there," she says and I plonk her hat on and say "I bet it was" and Mavis J. starts screaming she's lost her trousers and somebody must have seen them somewhere.

Mrs Warren finds Mavis's trousers behind the back of the bus with the lads, which is where they're changing. Just behind a sheet Mr K. is holding in the air.

Personally, I think Mr Kendal will be lucky to see his band ready this side of Christmas but in the end, we were all ready and we trooped off the bus where Mrs Warren nearly had a heart attack because Karen Green had put so much make-up on everybody's face, we looked as if we'd all turned into Italians overnight.

Maria is Italian, so she was O.K. About the only one who was though. Mrs Warren was going round with a box of tissues for half an hour, rubbing as much stuff off as she could.

We all lined up and Mr Kendal brought our instruments round and then he brought the brush handles E. H. had turned into maces and we picked them up real careful.

"Go steady with them" he says. "Remember the silver bits are only glued on." And we nodded and promised to be careful and then we all lined up ready to start marching.

There were about eight other bands and you should just have seen them. They were enormous. There were thousands of lasses in them and they had sashes wrapped round them and these sashes were covered in badges and some were silver and some were gold. Some had 'First' and some had 'Second' written on them and one girl had about six million badges entirely with 'First' written on them.

Mavis Jarvis looks at them and dashes back into the bus and comes out with her badge pinned onto her uniform jacket. This badge just says "What?"

We all thought it looked stacks better than anybody else's badge.

"Why 'What?'?" Mrs Warren says, when she sees M. J.'s badge but old Mavis, she just says "What?" and Mrs Warren sighs and says, "Very well, Mavis," and doesn't say any more.

Mr Kendal comes up to me and he says, "Now, Lily, you have to lead the band and

I'm looking to you to make a good job of it. Have you got your string on?" and I show him my string, which is tied to my right hand, and he says, "Good girl. When I blow this whistle, Lily" – and he shows me his whistle as if I didn't know what a whistle was – "When you hear this whistle, then I want you to blow *your* whistle and start marching. Right?"

I said, "Right," because we've done all this. I have a whistle the same as Mr K.'s and when I want the band to march, I whistle once and when I want them to slow down or stop or anything else, then I whistle for that as well.

Mr Kendal rushes off and about three seconds later, I hear the whistle, so I blow my whistle and we all start marching. All the other bands have gone because we were put on last. When we get out into the High Street, there's a great crowd of people standing clapping.

I was all right till I saw them and then my legs started shaking and I took a deep breath like my Gran's always told me to when I'm nervous. I wish she hadn't because when I took that deep breath, I forgot I'd still got the whistle in my mouth (which you have to keep there all the time on account of how you have your hands full with your

Mam's brush handle), and the whistle whistled.

Whooooh, it went, instead of Wheeeeeeh, because I was breathing in instead of breathing out but that didn't matter to our band. They know their orders and when they hear this whistle, they all come to a dead stop.

I didn't realise they had until I thought it had gone very quiet all of a sudden and you're not allowed to turn round and see where they are so the very next shop window I went past, I turned my head sideways and looked in it and all that looked back was me.

By this time, Mr K's caught up with me and he's hissing "Stop, Lily. Stop." And so I stop and mark time. My legs were going like pistons, I can tell you, and I still couldn't hear anybody coming and then Mr K. goes, "Blow your whistle, Lily. Blow your whistle and get them moving."

I blew my whistle and I heard them coming and it sounded like an elephant stampede. They were in that much of a hurry to catch up with me, they came down that road at about forty miles an hour.

In fact, they went that fast, Michelle Parish and Samantha Collins who were carrying the banner, had to swerve to one side when they got to me and before I could blink, I was at the back.

Mr Kendal was dancing up and down on the pavement and he was going "Lily. Lily. Get in FRONT of them, Lily," and that was easier said than done, because they were all over the place and we were supposed to keep to one side of the road to let the cars go past on the other.

Young Stella must have turned one car driver into a white haired old man because all at once she goes, "Wait for me," and launches herself into the wrong bit of road.

If it hadn't been for the fact that old M. J. was so close to Stella, she couldn't see her over the top of her drum, Stella would have been squashed flat. As it was, Mavis J.'s drum shoved her out of the way and sent her straight into Mr Kendal's arms, who had done a leap off that pavement which was every bit as good as you see gazelles doing on T.V. in Africa.

No car would ever dare run over Mavis. It'd never move again and this car swerved right over to one side and ended up practically in a shop window.

There were some bobbies there and they didn't like that. The last I saw of that car, there was about three bobbies marching down on it and they'd ALL got their notebooks open and their pencils sharpened.

I packed in trying to keep in step and just

ran straight down past all that stupid band and got back in front. I blew on my whistle as hard as I could and everybody stopped dead and I waited till Mr K. had sorted them all out and then we started marching again.

All the other bands had disappeared by now and all the people had gone with them. There was only one bobby car with two policemen in it, and one with a walkie-talkie and a bike, and us.

It was red hot and we hadn't been going five minutes when Stella started shouting, "Mrs Warren. Mrs Warren," and Mrs W. was walking in front of me and she was trying to pretend she hadn't heard anything, but young Stella wasn't going to have that.

"Mrs Warren. Mrs Warren," she shouts. "I want to go to the lav." and if Mrs W. could have dropped straight down a crack in the pavement, I think she would have done.

She went pinker than she was already but she slowed down and shouted to Stella "There's no lav. till we get to the field, Stella," and then Stella went wah, wah, wah, and one of these bobbies, the one with the bike, he said, "Come on, put her on the cross bar," and he cycled past me with Stella sat on his cross bar, switching his radio off and on.

She got a lift right up to the field, did that Stella, but by the time we got there, we were all like melted ice creams and Mr Kendal wouldn't even talk to us.

Mrs Warren says, "Never mind. You did very well, really, to say it was the first time on a public march."

Mr K. only said he'd seen centipedes, which have over a hundred feet EACH, march better than we had and we only had two each to control.

"You'd think," he goes, "you'd think two feet wouldn't be too much to manage, wouldn't you?" and Mrs W. bought us all a drink of orange juice and told us to sit down until we had to parade round the field.

I was sat there, wishing I was dead, and minding my own business, when Mavis J., she comes up and says, "I see you've got your string on your left hand, as usual." And I looked at this string and I says, "Left hand? That's not my left hand. That's my right hand."

"That's your left hand," Mavis J. says. "I think I know the difference between left and right, which is more than you do." And then she went off and before I could ask Karen, Mr K. was shouting, "Right, band. Into line. Fall in, please. If you don't mind. Come along now," and in five seconds flat, I had to blow my whistle and we were all marching out onto that field.

7

Deirdre Summers gets left over

Mr Kendal asked me if I was keeping this book properly and I said yes, and he said, "Did you write down about the band contest then?" and I nodded and he said, "Tear that bit out before you let me read it. I don't think I could survive that again," and he stomped off all scowling and mad.

That doesn't make much change though. He's been scowling and mad since last Sunday.

My Gran, she says, "What made you turn the wrong way, Lily?" and I says to her, "It was Mavis Jarvis. She told me I'd got that string on the left hand and it was on my right," and then I burst into tears because there's only so much anybody can stand and I've taken as much as I'm going to.

The next person who asks me which is my left hand and which my right is going to get both of them straight in their teeth and they can sort it out for themselves.

When we got on that field, right in the middle of it there was stood this huge man and he was wearing a kilt and him and two others just like him were judging the bands.

Of course, Stella didn't know it was called a kilt when a man wears one and I heard her going, "Look, that mister's wearing a skirt" and she starts shouting, "Mam! Mam! Mam, this mister's wearing a skirt" and I could see Mrs Green out the corner of my eye trying to take cover behind a newspaper but nothing was going to stop Stella then.

She suddenly shoots straight in front of me and runs up to this bloke and throws her arms round his knees. 'Course, that's the last thing he's expecting and he staggers back, trying to keep his balance but before he can do any of this, Tiny bounds out and grabs this piper's kilt between his teeth and he's going gggrowwl, yuk, yuk, snarlll.

Mr Kendal was standing at the top of the field facing us and all I saw was him slapping his hand over his eyes – again (one of these days he's going to give himself a black eye for sure). Then Mrs Warren was on the field and she whipped Stella up and stuck her back into line and dragged Tiny off behind her.

There were two grooves right down the

field where Tiny went. He didn't go willingly. You could hear him going woof, woof, and yip, and then he got slapped into the bus and the doors shut on him and he spent the rest of the afternoon with his head hanging out of a window licking anybody's ice cream cornet who didn't see him there first.

Even though we were marching on grass, I could practically hear young Stella crashing one foot down after the other and the big piper was trying to get his teeth into two straight lines so's everybody would know he wasn't going to hold it against us, but he kept forgetting and then his smile vanished and he looked like a walking thundercloud.

That Stella. She'll get us all hung one of these fine days.

All this time, of course, I'm standing there keeping the band marking time till we get Stella back into line and once everything was sorted out, off we went again.

Mr Kendal had said, "When you get to the middle of the field, turn right by the piper and march straight down past him," and I thought, that's easy, and I looked at the piper and turned my head smartly, like we've been taught to do, although it nearly takes your head clean off your neck, and I was just going to turn when this piper moved.

He went hop, skip, jump, and out of sight, just like a rabbit in a field.

I didn't know what the heck to do then. My eyeballs must have been spinning round like catherine wheels because I was trying to get this piper back into sight.

Rather than turn the wrong way, I didn't do anything. We just kept on marching.

I could hear Mr K. shouting, "RIGHT, Lily. Turn RIGHT." And I wondered which hand was right and I looked at the string on my hand and I thought, "That M. Jarvis was having me on," and I was just going to turn the same way as the string, when suddenly, this piper leapt into view again.

He was standing on the other side of me now, so I knew Mavis J. had been right after all and I'd made a mistake.

Without wasting any more time because we'd nearly run out of field, and I was practically nose to nose with Mr K., I blew my whistle and turned sharp right and this piper stared at me marching towards him and his mouth dropped open. This is a grown man I'm telling you about. Standing there catching flies when he was supposed to be judging our band.

"The other way, girlie," he growled and I threw my mace up in the air, caught it, whipped it round my head and the tennis ball

covered in silver paper that was never going to come off no matter what, it went zip, zip, straight into that piper's mouth, just as if I'd been playing marbles.

"Erk!" he went and his hand went flying up to check all his teeth were still there and that this lump of silver hadn't split his mouth open, because one thing you can't do with a cut mouth and that's play the bagpipes.

That put me off my stroke, I can tell you, and I can tell you something else as well. If looks could kill, I'd be pushing up daisies now, not writing this.

This piper, he went growl, "What band arrr ye, lassie?" And I went, "Please Sir, the Welly Band, Sir, please." And he goes, "The Welly Band, ay? Ah'll remaimbair thut."

I could feel myself going cross-eyed by

now but I thought this is no place to hang around so I kept our band on the move and we went down the side of this piper.

You could tell he hadn't cut his lip because he kept going growl, growl, only with a lot of r's, all the time we were marching.

I said to Mr Kendal after, "Look, Mr Kendal, I was in the right. I went down the side of the piper like you said. It was him that was wrong, he was standing too near the edge of the field." But all Mr K. would say was, "I'll never be able to lift my head up again."

The thing was, see, there wasn't enough room for the band to go down the right side of the piper so half of us ended up among the people watching us.

"Gerroff me fingers," I could hear, and, "What the . . . ?" and, "Where do you think you're going?" So I turned left this time and we marched back to the middle of the field and Mavis J. was playing her drum really good and I threw my stick up in the air and just happened to notice that my white gloves were pitch black.

Boot polish! E. Harris had used boot polish and now it was hot, it was all coming off on my gloves.

After that though, it was simple. We went round and round that field marching and playing and we even stopped a couple of times. Once, I led the banner with Michelle Parish and Samantha Collins and also Stella Green off on our own, like Mr K. taught us, and the rest of the band did a very good piece where they marched up and down each other's line, round in a circle and then got together again.

At the end of it, there was only Deirdre Summers and her triangle left over and she said she didn't mind a bit.

Deirdre just stood and watched the others and she said, "I'm not kidding, I reckon it was the best band there," and none of us could understand why Mr K. shouted at her afterwards.

"What were you doing?" he yells at D. Summers. "Playing musical chairs?" Then Deirdre started sulking and she didn't speak to anybody till we got home and then it was only to say, "Rotten lot," before she went into their house.

Mr Kendal says there shouldn't have been anybody left over but with so many people in the band, I wasn't surprised to see old Deirdre standing there like she did.

After the marching, there was the judging and these three pipers, they kept shouting names out and all these other bands were shouting and cheering and kids were running up and getting a badge for this and a badge for that and then running back and sitting down, and our names weren't called at all, and it just made me sick.

Not until it came to the drummers was our band mentioned and then the piper shouted, "The Welly Band. Mavis Jarvis." And old M. J. leapt to her feet and she's down that field like a bullet.

"Welly Band?" says Mr K.

We just sat there dumbfounded (that means quiet) until Mr K. suddenly yelled, "Cheer then, drat it. Cheer." So we cheered. "Hip, Hip, Hooray" we went and Mavis J. came back with this badge winking and glinting in her hand.

"FIRST" it said on it and she pinned it onto her sash and Mr K. said, "We're all proud of you, Mavis. Very proud indeed," and he bought her an ice cream.

Then he turns round to us and he roars, "Harris," meaning E. H. so naturally, old E. H. didn't move not even an eyelid and Mr K. snorted a bit and then he roared, "E. H.," and E. Harris sauntered to the front and Mr Kendal said, "What have you got to say to that?" and he points to me and Donna Stone and Claire Parkin, who all have maces.

When I look at Donna and Claire, I see they're as black as the back of a fireplace. All the polish has come off their brush handles as well and Karen Green, she says to me, "You look real mucky," and so E. Harris gets all fed up and goes, "I did my best. If they weren't such half wits, that would have been more than enough," and I see that Donna's lost her tennis ball wrapped in E. H.'s Mam's cooking foil off the end of her mace as well.

Mr K. sighed and then he looked at old M. J.'s badge and he cheered up a bit and he says, "Well, that's a FIRST anyway," and there's a silver cup to go with it and he tells Mavis he'll take care of that, thank you very much, and it takes both him and Mrs Warren to get this silver cup out of old Mavis's hand.

"Gerroff," she's going. "It's my cup." And Mrs Warren is saying, "No, Mavis dear. It belongs to the band." And in the end, E. H. tickled her and she dropped this silver cup, in order to plant E. H.'s teeth in the grass, and Mr Kendal scooped it up and put it in his pocket.

"In the morning," Mr K. says, "you can have it for a whole week." But old Deadly Nightshade, she says, "I want to show my Mam and Dad it." But Mr K. just says, "No, can't be done." He won't give it up, not even when Mr Jarvis tells him he'll have the police on him for wrongful possession.

"You do that," Mr Kendal says. "But just

remember who runs this band. Who made this band. Who put this band together." And he's all hot and bothered and Mrs Warren, she's standing behind Mr K. going, "That's right. You tell them. You couldn't be more correct."

So, that was it. Our first band competition.

All I can say is that I shall be glad when I'm too old for things like this.

E. H. says, "We've got a gig on tonight. Do you want to come?" I looks at him and says, "A gig? What's a gig?" and Gary Smith says, "We're playing at the Youth Club."

"You are?" I says and E. H. nods and goes, "That Mr Johnson, he realised where he went wrong. He booked us for tonight. E. H. and the Dead Beats. Only trouble is," E. H. goes, "only trouble is, I'm a Dead Beat short on account of how Scott Watson won't come back with his ukelele."

That is because the last time they played at the Youth Club, Scott Watson's ukelele got stuffed up his jumper because he would only play George Formby songs and pretend to be leaning on a lamp-post, when E. H. and Gary Smith were playing 'Big Toe Boogie Rock' and singing to it at the same time.

E. H. and Gary got thrown out as well.

They're very hard to please at the Youth Club.

"I was wondering," E. Harris goes on, "if you'd like to be a Dead Beat for a night?"

"Erk," I went.

"What I'm planning, see," says E. Harris, "I'm planning a heavy rock number. Real heavy, man."

"And cool," Gary Smith says.

"And cool," E. H. goes. "Yeah, man. Dead cool," and then he coughs and says, "Where was I?"

"Dead cool," I says and E. H. goes, "Yeah, cool. Anyway, what I had in mind, I thought we'd do a real heavy scene, man, like, you know, with Death on the stage."

"Death?" I says.

"Death," E. H. nods. "Yeah."

"And who did you have in mind to be death?" I asked him and he nods his head up and down and says, "Kinda . . . you."

And then he tells me how I have to go home and put the boot polish he's got left over from our brush handles all over my face and arms and legs and then get into an old coal sack.

"With the coal still in it?" I ask E. H. and old Gary, he says, "How would you do that? Here, that's an idea," and I have to kick him before he comes to his senses.

Anyway, there I'll be, black from top to toe, wearing an old coal sack and every time

111

E. H. finishes a song, I jerk about a bit and go "Yeah, Yeah."

I thought they must take me for a dope but I says to E. H. "You'll have to ask my Gran," because I know my Gran'll go daft when she hears about me playing Death.

"O.K." E. H. says. "Right on." so we go to my Gran's flat and E. H. and old Gary tell her all about this Death bit and at the end, my Gran says, "Now I'm sorry, E. H., but Lily can't go on that stage covered in shoe polish and clad in a coal bag. No, no, she's too young."

So, E. Harris, he looks at my Gran and then he says, "Hey, man," and my Gran goes cough, cough, so E. Harris starts again and he says, "Hey, Gran, I don't suppose you'd do it, would you?" The last I saw of them, they were running down them steps as fast as they could go.

Then my Gran looked at me and she said, "Judging by the colour of you, you've been in a coal sack already." Then it was bath time.

Mr Kendal said the band would have to shut down in the winter.

Well, roll on winter.

8

Horses don't eat cannon fodder

Mr Kendal tackled me about the Welly Band last meeting. He goes, "Here, young Lily, was it you told them we was called The Welly Band?" and I says, "Erm. Erm." And he says, "I thought it was."

Well, the upshot of it all is that we're going to be called The Welly Band proper.

Mrs Green, when she heard about it, she said, "That means a new banner will have to be sewn," but the one we had was Granny Green's Union Jack with our name on it and Granny Green says she wants her flag back, anyway, on account of how we all stalk about practically stark naked underneath it and if Mr K. thinks that's a fitting thing to do in front of the Union Jack, which, as everybody knows is practically the same thing as the Queen sitting there (?), then she doesn't know what the world's coming to and she wants her flag back like double quick.

Mr Kendal says we're to have a scarlet banner with our name written in gold, to match our uniforms. I should think that will be about the best flag anybody's ever seen but there's this problem.

"We've no money to buy the materials with," Mrs Green says. "I'll make the flag free and me and my friends will sew the name and everything on it but we have to have the materials first."

Mr Kendal goes, "Hmmmm. Yes, I see your point," and then he tells Mrs Warren it's time we had another fund raising event.

Mrs W. goes, "You're not going to put another concert on, Mr Kendal, I do hope?" Mr K. shakes his head and says, "Once bitten, twice shy, Mrs Warren." Then he goes, "No, I thought we'd have a collection day in the town."

Mr Kendal had to ring up the police and all sorts of things so that he can get permission to have this collection day.

Next thing, he's saying, "Now, we want volunteers to take the tins round the town," and he goes point, point, point and me, E. H., Karen Green and just about everybody who was there end up with a tin in our hands. Even my Mam and my Gran get a tin each.

My Gran says, "Well, Lily, you'll just have

to stand with me because I'm not going into that town on my own, not carrying a tin, I'm not."

When Saturday came, it was pouring rain. You never saw rain like it. It was coming down like clothes props.

My Gran says, "We'll catch our death of colds in this lot," and we were stood in front of the Co-op for so long, it's a wonder a traffic warden didn't stick a ticket on us.

Then my Gran saw a man she knew and he came up and he says, "Now then, Sarah, what are you collecting for?" and my Gran tells him.

"It's this band they're in, Tom," she says. "They go marching and things like that. It's very good for them. They need uniforms, though, and instruments and it all costs money."

"Uniforms!" Tom says. "Marching! Well, Sarah, I'd have thought we'd had enough of uniforms in't last war."

"Those days have gone," my Gran says. "These are just children," and she looks at me, all kind, sees what I'm doing and then slaps my hand. "How many times have I told you not to scratch your head?"

Then she looks at this Tom again and she gets that drippy voice on, which was missing when she all but took the hand off from the

115

end of my arm, and she says, "Only children, Tom. If we can't help little children, who can we help?" and I stick my hands in my pockets to save them getting rattled again.

When kids hit you, it's because they want to. When grown-ups hit you, it's because they're 'being cruel to be kind'. They both hurt just the same.

I says to my Gran, "How are you being kind when you're being cruel?" And she says, "I'm cruel when I hit you," and I thought, if she knows she's being cruel, why hit me, but then my Gran goes on, "and I'm being kind because I'm stopping you scratching your head in front of everybody so they won't all point at you and say you've been dragged up."

I says, "Why can't you just tell me not to scratch my head?" And my Gran, she goes, "Ohhhh! Out of my way, child. I've got too much to do to stand and argue with you." That's my Gran, who's supposed to love me!

This Tom, he's talking to my Gran for ages and he's getting wilder and wilder and all upset and in the end, he goes stamping off and my Gran says, "Well, I always said he never got over that war wound of his," and she shakes her tin so hard, she gets a lot of people putting money in it, because they daren't walk past.

My Gran goes home at dinner time and E. Harris comes and stands with me.

"Blinking job this is," E. H. says, and he stands in the Co-op doorway so that none of his pals will see him.

"You'll not get much there," I tell him, but he does, because every time anybody goes into the Co-op, he opens the door for them and they're all in such a state of shock, they get money out for him without thinking about it.

E. H. is much cleverer than anybody realises.

He says, "Just call me Genius and one day, somebody will write a book about me."

I says to him, "Don't look at me," because this book is enough for one lifetime, I reckon. There isn't time to write any more.

E. H. goes, "Think about it, Piccalilli," and then whips his head sideways and smiles.

I walk round to face him so I can talk to him and he goes zing, and his head's gone to the side again and he smiles again.

"What you doing, E. H.?" I ask him at last because he makes me jump always whipping his head this way and that and grinning for no reason at all.

I told my Gran about it and asked her if she knew if there was anybody who'd ever gone mad in E. H.'s family.

"Not as I know to," she said, "not as have a certificate for it, anyway," she goes on, and laughs.

I reckon E. H. will be the first at this rate.

E. H. though, he says, "That's my best side, dope."

"What is?" I says and E. Harris, he goes, "Oh," moan, "girls are thick, thick, thick." He points at his face and goes jab, "That. My best side. My best PROFILE. Ready for when I'm a SUPERSTAR."

Well, what can you say to that? As far as I can see, he's got just as many spots on his left side as he has on his right.

You can't tell Elvis Harris anything though because he knows it all. Even if you didn't, you couldn't tell him about his spots. He'd flatten you.

I stand there and everything is wet through but my tin is getting heavier and heavier and I'm thinking how pleased Mr K. will be when we empty it out and find about a hundred pounds in it, when there's this noise.

De-de-dum dah de-de-dum and it's my Gran's friend, Tom, and he's walking down the road holding a big stick with a piece of cardboard on top of it and he's playing a trumpet all at the same time. Very clever.

"What's the notice say?" E. H. goes and we don't have long to wait before we find out because this Tom, he comes and stands right next to me.

"Here," I says to him. "I was here first." But Tom goes, "Now then, you shouldn't be collecting money for bands at your age," and I read his poster then.

It says, DOWN WITH CHILDREN'S BANDS on one side and on the other it goes BANDS TODAY – CANNON FODDER TOMORROW.

"What's cannon fodder?" I asks, and E. H. says, "It's what horses eat."

"Is it?" I says. But Tom goes, "You're partly right there, son, and partly wrong. Horses eat fodder, right enough, but it's guns that eat men. Armies of men. Armies of marching men, they becomes cannon fodder, see, for the guns eat their lives away."

"But we're not armies of men, marching men," I say. And Tom nods his head and says, "You're not today, but if you keep on dressing up in uniforms and marching and doing what you're told, turn right, turn left, quick march, by the time you're twenty one, you'll be cannon fodder all right and nobody'll even have to train you."

I thought blimey and E. Harris, he looks at Tom for a long time and Tom looks back at him and they don't say a word and I wonder if they're playing Staring Out but they can't be because in the end, E. H. says, "I never thought of it like that before," and Tom goes "Then you should, young man, because when you put that khaki uniform on for real, you're halfway to being cannon fodder already."

Then my Gran's friend goes on his own march through our town.

E. Harris says, "Here, I'm off home. You can take my tin." And I says to him, "Take you, own tin. What do you think I am, your slave?" And he goes, "You heard what Tom said, didn't you? The very next war and you'll be expecting me to fight for you, won't you?"

"Who will?" I says. And E. H. goes, "You will."

"Huh," I tell him. "If I need any fighting done for me, I shan't come to you," and E. H. whips his head to one side, smiles like he thinks his favourite pop star smiles, crooked (really stupid lads are), and he sneers "No?" I says, "No. I'll get Mavis Jarvis. She's bigger than you," and that finishes E. H. off.

He won't speak to me for a fortnight but I shan't mind about that, you can bet on it.

I'm really fed up of people speaking at me all the time.

Next thing, Mr K. appears like Aladdin out of his lamp and he's going, "Where's

Tom?" and I think this morning I never even knew there was a Tom and now here I am, people walking up to me in the street and saying, "Where's Tom?"

"Where's Tom?" Mr Kendal says again. And I say, "He went thataway," and point up the street and Mr K. leaps off up the street after this Tom.

Then Mavis J. comes rushing up and she says, "'Ere, fish face, guess what?" And I goes, "What, glass eyes?" And she says, "The bobbies have took Mr Kendal and that funny old bloke to prison," and she says Mr K. and Tom started rowing in the street and it all ended up with Tom picking up his poster and hitting Mr K. on the head with it.

"Well," Mavis Jarvis goes. "Mr Kendal's head went straight through this poster and then he got mad and tried to push that bloke's trumpet through a letter box, spotty."

"That wouldn't be easy, frog feet," I said and Mavis J. shook her head.

"It weren't," she said. Mr Kendal had to jump on it in the end and then he fell off it and twisted his ankle and that's when the bobbies came and took 'em both away, ugly chops."

I stared at old Poison Ivy and I was so fed up and wet through and cold, I just reached out and bashed her one, straight on the nose.

"How does that strike you, Mavis?" I said and she opened her eyes wide, till she looked exactly like that monster who was made out of bits and pieces, then she lifted her arm up in the air, folded her hand into a fist and brought it straight down on top of my head.

"The same way as that strikes you" she goes, and I was stood there trying to keep my knees straight, which they would not do, and then my Gran came and she slapped both of us.

"Both ought to know better," she snapped and took us home.

Mavis Jarvis went into her flat and we went into my Gran's.

"I want my Mam," I said. And my Gran goes, "I want never gets." Then my Mam came in all cold and wet and she says, "Come on, Lily. Let's get off home and settle ourselves in front of that telly for the night," and I didn't have to sleep with my Gran, like I do when my Mam's on nights at the factory.

When it was bedtime, my Mam looked at the clock and I looked at her and she smiled and waved her hand in the air. "Blow it," she said. "What's bedtime?" and I got to stay up till midnight and then, me and my Mam, we went up to bed at the same time and it was all very good.

I don't know where my Dad is and I wouldn't recognise him if I saw him, anyway, not even though I do know he has wavy brown hair, blue eyes, a straight thin nose and long lips. He's very tall and he has thin hands with a scar shaped like a half moon on his left one, which he did on a piece of glass when he was a little boy.

I wouldn't know him if I saw him and I wouldn't want to know him, either.

The only good thing that's happened for ever is that we collected enough money to pay for the banner for the band, and to buy two more kazoos and half of a second hand drum.

Mavis J. nearly had a fit when she heard

123

somebody else was getting a go at a drum, even though it was only half a one.

"I'm the drummer," she goes. And Mr K. says, "We need more than one drummer, my girl. You're the big drum."

"And the big mouth too," Karen Green says, and Mr Kendal told us to be quiet because he had something important to tell us.

"Mrs Warren and I," he says, and then he goes quiet. "Mrs Warren and I," he goes again. "We're going to be married and we'd like you all to come to the wedding."

Everybody was shouting and cheering then.

When I told my Gran, she says, "Well, just let's hope Mrs Warren doesn't meet a chimney sweep as well."

A wedding!

That'll be something to write about.

9

Mrs Green's sheepskin rug comes in handy

E. Harris said we all ought to get together and practise The Wedding March and play it for Mr Kendal and Mrs Warren when they get married, so we met last Thursday and Mavis Jarvis says, "How does this Wedding March thing go, then?"

E. H. went Dom Dom Dom Dommmm, on his tin plates and says, "That's how it goes." And we all looked at each other and Karen Green says, "Oh, *that's* how it goes." Crash, crash, crash, crash, and she whips round to the band and shouts, "Right. Now you've all got the tune in your minds, let's rollllll." So everybody went bang, bang, bang, bang, or blurt, blurt, if they were playing a kazoo, and Deirdre Summers went ting, ting, on her triangle and that was it.

E. Harris says, "Listen, stupid." And Karen Green says, "We've listened to you once already and look what came out of it.

Just a load of old noise," and I thought for a minute Elvis Harris was going to hit her.

I was ready to go and help him because Karen Green can be very fierce when she wants. She doesn't think of anything when she's mad, she just starts fighting and E. H., well, he says afterwards, "She nearly pushed me beyond my limits, she did. Me, who's never hit a lass before," and I had to calm him down.

I said, "It's not in your nature to hit a girl, E. H." And he goes, "You're right, Piccalilli, it isn't," and then it took me all my time not to hit him. One thing I really hate is being called Piccalilli.

Anyway E. H. whistled The Wedding March and I says to him, "Here, isn't that a bit slow for a wedding? Walking at that rate, they'll be drawing their old age pension before they get as far as the altar." But E. H. says people have to walk slow on account of how everybody walks slow in church.

"You never hear them singing fast hymns, do you?" he says and I shake my head, because you don't. The only quick hymn I can think of is 'Onward, Christian Soldiers' but even in that one, when you get to the Soldiers bit, they all lie down and die.

Deirdre Summers said they carry smoking candles in their church as well, that they swing from side to side and they smell really nice.

"It would be great if we could do that," she goes, and everybody says yes, it would, and Gary the Dead Beat, he's told to get a smoking candle that smells nice and something to swing it in and we'll have that for this wedding too.

"This is going to be some wedding," E. H. says. And we all nod but we didn't realise then just how much of a wedding it was going to be.

Well, we practised that Wedding March until we were going in circles with it and then Karen Green says, "We'll wait till they come out of the church and we'll play it for them as they walk down the path."

That sounded a very good idea to us all and by the Friday night, the day before Mr K. and Mrs W. got married, we were perfect.

My Gran says, "Being given a ticking-off by the Police isn't a very good way to start married life," because Mr Kendal and Tom, they were hauled off to the Police Station and got a real telling-off for causing a disturbance in the High Street.

'Causing a disturbance' is having a fight and when you reckon how old Mr K. and Tom are, it's a wonder they didn't end up in hospital and not the Police Station.

Tom has a bad leg and a policeman in a police car had to take him right the way home because this leg wouldn't bend in the middle at all. "It just seized up," he told my Gran. And my Gran said, "Fancy two grown men fighting in the middle of a main street." But Tom said he would do it again, although the policeman who took him home told him he wasn't to.

"Go on like this," he said, "and you'll end up with both legs not being able to bend in the middle and then how will you go on?"

Tom said then he'd get a pair of stilts but the policeman didn't think that was a bit funny.

"Not funny at all," he says.

Well, we practised that Wedding March until we could all play it in our sleep and Mavis J. said, "It sounds to me as if that's what you are doing, as well," and Karen Green told M. J. just to play her drum, if she didn't mind and if she did, had she ever thought about trying the drumsticks in her mouth for size?

"Whichever way you put them, they should fit," she says.

Old M. J. didn't reckon much to that and she says, "I haven't tried them in *my* mouth but I'll try them in *yours*, if you want," and she tried to get one past Karen G's teeth but it didn't fit, not at all, and it didn't fit because old Karen, she whipped this drumstick out of M. J.'s hand and rocketed across that field with it.

Mavis J. looks at Karen vanishing with her drumstick and she starts shouting, "Come back with my drumstick," but Karen wouldn't. Not until she got to the river, that is, and then she threw this drumstick as far as she could and even though we all searched high and low for it, we couldn't find it again.

E. H. was really mad. I've never seen him as mad as that before. He was so mad he started cleaning his teeth with the wrong end of a match and it burst into flames. That didn't make him any happier, I can tell you.

Zip, he went with this match, and whoosh went all the flames. That put paid to his moustache for another fortnight, which you cannot see at all but which E. H. says was growing a treat, all ready for the wedding.

"And what are we going to do now, stupid?" he said to old Karen. And she said, "I don't know and I don't care," but she got worried after a bit and went home to see if her Mam would lend us a bit of her sheepskin rug which she has in her bedroom at the side of her bed. And her Mam said, "No, certainly not."

E. H. goes, "That's put the kibosh on

everything, then. No drumstick, no big drum," and Mavis J. went home crying real tears which were pouring down her face.

"My drum," she was going. "My poor drum," and we all felt sorry for her. Well, as sorry as you ever feel for Mavis J. I can feel sorry for her as long as I don't think about it but when I think about it, I remember all the times she's thumped me or bashed somebody else littler than her, and then I stop feeling sorry pronto.

Anyway, Karen Green goes back home and cuts a corner off her Mam's sheepskin rug which she says her Mam'll never notice and E. H. wraps this round a stick which Gary the Dead Beat brought out of his little brother's building set and it looked just like the real thing, almost.

Mavis J. tried it out and it went bang, bang, the same as the other stick and she said it was O.K.

"What about twirling it, though?" she goes. "Will I be able to twirl it?" and E. Harris says, "Twirl it? Twirl it? I should just think you will be able to twirl it. Why, I've put that sheepskin on that well, it'll never come off no matter what," and Mavis Jarvis burst into tears again when she heard this.

E. H. goes, "Wassamatterwiver? Wassamatterwiver?" and Mavis J. just went sob, sob, but I knew. That's exactly what E. Harris said about the tennis ball he stuck on the end of my mace and look where that ended up, in a strange man's mouth, that's where that ended up.

Mavis Jarvis's drumsticks have this silver rope on them and they hang from her wrists and when she marches, she goes twirl, twirl, with the drumsticks, when she's not banging them on her drum that is.

Sometimes, she even twirls them above her head and then brings them down, crash, crash, on the drum. She's very good at it. That's why she won that First.

Now, she walks across the field and starts twirling her drumstick and the one E. H. made her and wheeee, off flies Karen Green's Mam's sheepskin carpet and it goes bounce bounce on the grass and Mavis Jarvis goes erk and falls down backwards and she says, "I wish I was dead, I do." And everybody's going, "Yers, so do we," and then she gets up and starts hitting them she can reach with the one drumstick she's got left.

"This is no laughing matter," E. Harris says but there isn't even a smile to be seen so why he said that, I don't know. Even Mavis J. stayed miserable, though she clouted at least twelve of the band with her last drumstick.

In the end, everything was sorted out and

E. Harris mended M. J.'s drumstick and when we left the field on Friday night, Karen Green goes, "Right, band. We'll meet outside the Church tomorrow morning at ten o'clock," and we were all looking forward to it ever so much.

10

What Gary pinched from the gas man

I must say that Mr K.'s and Mrs Warren's wedding was the very best wedding I have ever been to and when I asked Mr Kendal if I should write about it in the band book, he said, "Put it all down, Lily. I shall treasure that book."

"And so shall I," Mrs Warren said, so here I am, putting it all down.

First thing, on Saturday morning, I went down to the shop to fetch my Mam her comic, which has ladies on the front of it and knitting patterns inside, and why they put knitting patterns in it I do not know because my Mam knitted one of these jumpers for me, it is in bright yellow wool with great bobbles on it and when I went out in it, everybody stared and Mavis Jarvis went, "A camel!" and pointed at me, and then shouts, "Gis a ride," and jumps on my back.

I can tell you this much, any camel Mavis Jarvis rides wouldn't have a hump on its back for long. She'd flatten anything. She flattened me. I went, "Ooooof!" and vanished into the pavement.

E. H. says, "There wasn't a hole and then there was and there you were, Piccalili, in it," and all I could see was sticky black tarmac because they'd just finished tarmacking our pavements and I was covered in tar.

E. H. takes one look at me and he says to Mavis J., "Oh, well done. Now look at her. How's she going to be in the band like that?" and M. Jarvis thinks about her day out in her band uniform going down the drain, almost like I did, and she starts brushing me down.

"It's no good doing that," E. Harris snarls. "That tar'll never come off." So Mavis Jarvis, she rushes home and tells her Mam what she's done and her Mam says, "Come into the kitchen, Lily. Let's see if I can get it off," and she used butter and turpentine and she was just eyeing a tin of paint stripper when my Mam comes looking for me.

"Home!" my Mam says, jerking her head and then she says to Mrs Jarvis, "You weren't going to use that on her, were you?" meaning the paint stripper, and Mrs Jarvis said it worked very well on their Charles – named after Prince Charles like E. Harris is named after Elvis Presley. I just hope this Prince Charles doesn't pick his nose like Charlie Jarvis does, else we're going to be all right when he's King – everybody'll be sending him hankies to put in his pockets. Granny Green sent some hankies to Buckingham Palace once, the round ones that my Mam told me about, and she edged them with hand-made lace and embroidered sixteen raised red crowns in the middle of one and sixteen blue ones in the middle of the other.

My Mam said, "Knock your nose off, they would. They were that big."

Well, my Mam got that tar off and then I went out again to get this magazine for her and when I got outside the flats, I heard this voice, "L-i-l-l-yyyyyyy," it went. "L-i-l-l-yyyyyy." And I looked up and there was Karen Green leaning out of her bedroom window.

"I can't come," she says. And E. H. who just happened to be there as well, he went, "What?" And Karen says, "I can't come." Mavis Jarvis, who ought to be a genie in a lamp, she's that good at appearing where she's not wanted, she goes, "You've got to come." But Karen says, "My Mam found her rug."

E. H. says, "I thought you'd pushed it a bit further under the bed?" and Karen says she did, she did, but a great lump of fur came off this rug and got tangled up in her Mam's slippers and she'd got a rattle and been told she'd have to stop in for a whole week.

Elvis Harris, who is very clever, he says, "I'll go and see your Mam." First he went with me to get my Mam's magazine and then we went up the town and E. H. says, "Have you got any money on you?" and I says, "Fifty pence." And he says, "That'll do," and he put some money too as well and then he went and bought one red rose.

"See this," he says, and I nods because I'm looking straight at it. "This," he says, "is what's going to get Karen back into the band." Then he took this rose to Karen's Mam, who is nice but tough, and when Mrs Green saw this rose, she goes "Oh." tut "Well, all right then. Just this once," and she swatted E. H. round the head with her red rose and it didn't do it any good at all, I can tell you.

Waste of money it was.

I must say though, it made me think. I

shall remember all this when I meet my Dad. If he gives me a red rose, I shall snap it in two and throw it down and stamp on it.

"Not really," my Gran says. "You wouldn't really do that to an innocent flower, would you?" So I says, "Well, all right then. I'll snap it in two, tear all its petals off and then throw it down but I won't stamp on it," and my Gran sighed and goes, "That's better than nothing, I suppose."

Not as my Dad will give me a rose, anyway. So far, he hasn't given me anything but nothing and he still owes me tenpence from my tooth.

By ten o'clock, everybody was on the field dressed in their uniforms and we all shone and sparkled and then we went down to the church and made two lines outside the doors and waited till quarter past ten which was when Mr K. and Mrs W. would be coming out, E. H. reckoned.

"I should think fifteen minutes is long enough to get married in," he said.

We stood there and bang on quarter past ten, those big doors flew wide open and out comes sixteen thousand Brownies.

They looked at us as if we'd gone mad and we looked at E. Harris, who was going, "Well," cough, cough, "blow me." And "Who'd've thought it." And Mr Kendal and Mrs Warren weren't even in that Church, not at all.

"Well, where are they?" Mavis Jarvis shouts, her face all red, just as red as her uniform. "You great dope," she yells at E. H. "What you done with the wedding?"

E. H. rolls his eyes round and round and says, "This was just to test you," ha ha, and nobody laughed at all, not even me, although I usually laugh when E. Harris does but I didn't feel at all like it then, not with them Brownies rushing round practising reef knots on us with bits of rope.

E. H. shouts, "Fall in, band," and we all fall in. Mavis J. says, "The first river I see, Elvis Harris, you'll fall in. I'll push you in, that's what I'll do, I'll push you in and then I'll hit you on the head with my drumstick and then I'll . . . I'll . . . I'll go to the pet shop and buy a million piranha and put them in beside you and . . . and . . ." and then she had to stop for breath or have a heart attack instead.

Good thing God invented breathing if you ask me. Otherwise, we'd never get a minute's peace with M. J.

"Follow me," E. H. goes and starts marching and that band's stood there as if we'd all got our feet in glue and E. Harris has gone round the gates before he realises we're not there and he's shouting, "Left. Right. Left. Right," to three dogs, two little old women and Tom.

"Down with bands," Tom shouts and waves his poster at E. H.

"Where are you going with that?" Elvis Harris says and Tom goes, "Same place as you, my boy. Registry office." Then E. H. comes hurtling back and he says, "Well, come on then. What're you waiting for? Wedding'll be over by the time we get there at this rate."

We thought then that E. H. must know what he was doing so we followed him and he took us straight to the registry office.

"It'll be two minutes before they're out,"

somebody told E. H. so he led us into this big hall inside the registry office and we all stood there and E. H. goes, "Light the candles, Gary," and Gary the Dead Beat, he gets a match out of his pocket, scrapes it on the heel of his shoe and lights these candles which he has in a holey tin can on the end of a bit of string.

"Special candles, these," Gary the Dead Beat mutters, and just then Mr K. and Mrs W. comes out of the marrying room and Mr K. is smiling that much, it's a wonder his teeth don't meet round the back of his head.

You'd really need lips then, wouldn't you, to keep your head on. They'd be like a zip.

"Well," Mr K. says. "This is a nice surprise. Look at that, Gladys" (Mrs Warren) and Mrs W. looks at us and she says, "Lovely." Gary Smith walks down the middle of us, swinging his tin can with the candles in it and these candles suddenly go phut, phut, and thick white smoke pours out.

E. H. goes, "What's that?" Gary the Dead Beat, he says, "They're better than candles, E. H. They're what the gas men use to test the chimney when they put a gas fire in." E. H. goes "What?" but he can't say anymore because by that time, he can't even see Gary.

The whole room is full of this thick white

smoke and I can hear Gary going, "I borrowed them off the gas man, E. H. Just borrowed them. I'm going to give them back now, I think." Then all the doors start flying open and people are shouting, "Fire! Fire!" and E. H. roars at Gary the Dead Beat to take his candle outside.

"I can't find it," Gary goes. "I put it down a minute and now I can't find it."

Well, you never saw a wedding like that one. They had the fire brigade as well as a band, did Mr K. and Mrs W.

The police were there, as well. The registry office is straight across the road from the police station, you see, so when they saw all that thick white smoke coming from the doors and windows, the policemen piled across the road and dragged us all out.

By the time the fire brigade got there, it was all but over. One of the policemen had found Gary the Dead Beat's tin can and fetched it out but it had stopped smoking by then and Tom was marching up and down shouting, "Down with children's bands. Music today. War tomorrow" and then, when one of the policemen said, "Now, look, Grandad, let's have a bit of hush," he shouted, "Police State. Death of Free Country," and, "Down with Bands and Bobbies."

What a noise.

Mavis Jarvis is standing on the pavement roaring, "What about our band, then? What about our music?"

Mr Kendal explained everything to the policemen but that didn't stop them from taking us to the police station.

"You don't have to come with them," the policeman said to Mr Kendal. "We can fetch their parents." But Mr Kendal, he said, "Don't fetch their parents, Inspector."

"Sergeant," says the policeman.

"I'll come with them," Mr Kendal goes. "Me and Mrs . . . me and my wife, we'll come with them, Admiral."

"Sergeant," says the policeman. And then he goes, "All right, then, you come with them," and we all trailed across to the police station and we had to stand in a big room and this Sergeant told us all off.

"Where did this come from, anyway?" he says, and holds Gary the Dead Beat's tin can up in the air.

I heard old M. J. take a deep breath so I stamped on her foot and by the time she'd finished screeching, the Sergeant had told us we could go but that we'd better watch our steps in future. All of us.

"The faces of the lot of you are imprinted on my mind," he says and stares at us all in turn. Well, that took some time as well.

Deirdre Summers says, "Don't we get to be finger printed, Mister." And Mr Kendal went, "Shush, shush, Deirdre," and got us out of there before the Sergeant changed his mind.

When we got outside, Mr Kendal says, "Well, you meant well, anyway. It was a kind thought to come and play for us." E. H. says, "We've got a special tune to play for you." And Mr Kendal says, "I don't think we'd better hang around here any longer." And Mrs Warren goes, "You can play us into the reception, when we get to the Miner's Welfare," so that's what we did.

We all walked up to that hall and, halfway there, Karen Green goes scream, "Where's our Stella?" and we looked up hill and down dale and there was no Stella anywhere.

"She was with us at the church," Deirdre Summers says, playing her triangle, "because I saw her."

"In the middle of some of them kids in brown," Samantha Collins goes.

We all rush up to the church then and Mrs Warren, she says, "Hmmmmm," and starts rushing with us.

There are four main roads between the church and the registry office and Stella Green has about as much road sense as a hedgehog and you know what happens to poor old hedgehogs because of the horrible fast cars. They get squashed flat.

"Aaaagh!" Karen Green yells. "Don't let our Stella be squashed flat anywhere. My Mam'll kill me if she is."

"Two funerals," says old Mavis Jarvis.

Lucky for her, Mr Kendal didn't hear her.

Well, she wasn't (squashed flat, that is), not as we saw anyway. Mavis Jarvis (who cannot keep her big mouth shut) she says, "Perhaps the next road," and Karen Green nearly faints clean away and Mr K. tells M. J. that she won't be in the band much longer if she can't keep her tongue to herself.

"I'm only . . ."

"Well, don't" says Mr K.

When we got to the church, there's this great gang of Brownies standing around Stella and all you can see of her are the gold buttons down the front of her uniform. The rest of her is swathed in bandages.

"Just practising," these Brownies say when Karen drags their Stella away from them.

It took us a good ten minutes to get all the bandages off her but, Stella, she wasn't bothered. Those Brownies had been stuffing her full of liquorice allsorts and aniseed balls until her mouth was bright red and her teeth ready to drop straight out.

We were all ready for the reception, I can tell you. I felt as if I'd lived a hundred years and Mr Kendal, he said, "I never used to feel an old man. I didn't even feel an old man first thing this morning." Then he looked at Tom, who was trailing us everywhere with his placard and he says, "Come to the reception, Tom. There's a nice bit of grub there," and Tom looks at his placard, then at Mr K. and he says, "Can I bring it wi'me?" and Mr Kendal sighs and says, "You can bring it with you, lad," and he did.

When we got to the Miner's Welfare, E. H. says to Mr Kendal, "You and Mrs Warren stop out here a minute, Mr K. while we get ready," and inside the hall, there were dozens and dozens of guests all waiting for their dinner.

"Hurry up, young 'un," one of these guests says to E. Harris. E. Harris turns round and says, "These things can't be rushed, you know."

Fearless, Elvis H. is, fearless.

We were all in line in the end though and then the doors flew open and there stands Mr K. and Mrs W. and everybody starts cheering and flinging confetti and pink rose petals in the air and then Mr and Mrs Kendal start walking down the middle of our lines and we're playing The Wedding March.

I'm standing at the bottom of the hall, facing Mr K. and Mrs W. and I throw my stick up in the air and catch it and I watch them walking towards me and I think, there's something wrong here, and after a bit, I realise what it is.

Mr Kendal and Mrs Warren are walking in time with the band but they're going so slow, they have to have a long rest everytime they put a foot forward.

Step, rest, clunk, pause, they're going. Step, rest, clunk, pause.

"What's the matter then?" one of the guests shouts. "Dang" (I think it was dang) "Dang me, if they ain't playing that tune they play at funerals."

"All we need is a dozen soldiers to shoot in the air," Mrs Jarvis says, "and we'll be home and dry."

I just look at E. H. Wedding March! Trust him to get it muddled up with a funeral march.

There are times when I wonder about Elvis Harris and that was one of them.

Mr Kendal said afterwards, "It was very good music. So what if they had to wait a bit longer for their dinner. Do them good," and Mrs Kendal, she said, "Best music I've ever heard," and that was that.

My Mam and my Gran were at this

wedding too and then I turned round and there's a man standing with my Mam and I look and I know who it is.

It's my Dad, and he looks at me and I wait for him to whip a red rose out from behind his back but he does nothing of the sort. He just says, "Hello," and I say, "Hello," and then I says, "I'm off home now, Mam. I've got a lot of homework to do." And my Mam goes, "No, don't go. Stay with us for a bit. Your Dad wants to talk to you." But I don't stay.

I go away. Just like he went away from me.

My Gran walks home with me and she says, "No good running away, Lily. Things have a way of running after you. Better to stay and face them," and in the end, I say I'll see Mr Pickle at my Gran's, for I don't want to see him anywhere else.

"Not 'Mr Pickle' Lily," my Gran says. "He's your Dad, love. No matter when all's said and done, he's still your Dad."

"He's no Dad of mine," I tell her. "Not yet he isn't." Then my Gran says, "We'll have a nice cup of tea when we get in."

Personally, I wouldn't care if I never saw a nice cup of tea or Mr Pickle again.

Ever.

11

Fame at last

This is the end of the band book now. I've only got tonight to write about and a few other things and then that's it till next year.

When we went on the field last time to practise, Mr Kendal turned round and looked at us all and he goes, "Ah well," sigh. "I knew it was too good to last." And he stares at us and shouts, "Fall out all those in wellies," and Karen Green, she just leaned sideways until she fell straight down on the grass and then everybody else did the same. Bonk, bonk, bonk, we went, and Mr Kendal says, "Very funny, Karen," but there we were, lying on that field in our wellingtons and Mr Kendal goes, "Winter's coming, all right."

"Get up. Get up," he goes and when we're all standing in lines again, he says, "Now then, we've got one last important meeting," and everybody waits to hear what this important meeting is and Mr Kendal gets this letter out of his pocket and he tells us about it.

"This letter," he says, "this letter is asking us to play in a competition at a big dance in the Sports Centre. Now, there's three other bands taking part – big bands mind – not tatty ones. Big ones. Test our mettle they will, and this competition will be held in the interval of this dance, which is being run by all them pipers who gave Mavis here her First." Mavis Jarvis went smirk, smirk, breathed on her medal, polished it with her hanky and then pinned it back on her jumper. It ought to be pinned on her face, she never lets anybody forget she's got it.

Mr Kendal, who cannot be relied on because he thinks M. Jarvis is very good because she's got this stupid medal, he goes beam at Mavis and all but wipes away the tears from his eyes when he sees her, he goes, "There's a big silver cup to win, band, and not only that, there'll be a medal each, as well."

E. Harris says, "But them other bands have won hundreds of competitions, Mr Kendal." And Mr K. sighs and shakes his head and goes, "They may well have, my son, but this is one they're not going to win because," he goes, "because this time there's a sword dancing contest as well."

E. H. nearly faints clean away when he hears about this because there's one thing he cannot stand and that's the sight of blood. "Never been able to stand it since I nearly cut my entire leg off," he says and that was when he got scratched by a rusty nail and his Mam hauled him off to the hospital for an injection to stop him getting lockjaw.

"Your mouth, it closes," E. H. goes, "and it never opens again?"

"What, never?" Stella Green says. And E. H. Says, "Never."

Stella Green thinks about this, although thinking takes her a long time because she's only got a little brain yet, seeing as how she is five years old and her head hasn't finished growing.

"How do you eat then?" she goes and their Karen pushes her and says, "You don't eat, you great dope. You can't open your mouth, right? You don't eat, right? You get dead then, right?" and so little Stella starts walking round with her mouth wide open and that's not a pretty sight either, not when it's full of crisps and ice cream.

"Really dumb, she is," their Karen says, and pushes the half of their Stella's head above her mouth down and the half below her mouth up and Stella's mouth shuts with a crack like a trap closing.

If her tongue had been in the way, she'd have been short tongued for the rest of her life.

Mr Kendal goes, "When you've all quite finished," and E. H. shuts up and Mr K. says, "Nobody in the band has to do the sword dancing. What we have to do is play the music for it, and that's where we're going to get top marks, see."

"But sword dancing's very fast, isn't it, Mr Kendal?" Mavis Jarvis says and Mr K. nods his head.

"Very fast," he says. "So we're going to practise a very fast tune until we're perfect." And after that, he has us on that field night after night after night, until the night before the dance it was pitch black and we were still marching up and down and bits of the band kept disappearing because their Mams and Dads were fetching them home.

"Erm! I think it's time we stopped, Mr Kendal," Mrs Warren (Mrs Kendal) says. And Mr K. sighs and goes, "All right. All right. It is a bit dusky," and it's so dusky, you can't see your hand in front of your face.

Just then, we heard this ting, ting, and Mr K. goes, "What's that?" and it turns out to be Deirdre Summers and her triangle and she's practically three fields away.

"Come back here, Deirdre," Mr K. shouts

and old Deirdre, she wanders back and goes ting, "Can I go home now, please?" ting. Mr Kendal says, "Time for everybody to go home and now we'll just have to keep our fingers crossed because there's no more time to practise."

And tonight, Saturday, the bus came and we all got on it and all the Mams and Dads had bought tickets for this dance and we set off. It's only five minutes walk to the Sports Centre where the dance was going to be but Mr Kendal made us go in the bus because he said he wanted to be sure we all got there safe and sound.

When we got out at the other end, Mrs Warren (Mrs Kendal) counted all our heads and she went shriek, "There's one missing," and it turned out to be Awful Warning.

"I've seen Peggy Lane," Mavis J. goes. "She was here a minute ago. Wearing a green headscarf."

"A green headscarf?" Mrs Warren says, and turns round and grabs this little old woman wearing a green headscarf.

"What are you doing in that scarf, Elizabeth Lane?" Mrs Warren shouts, and tears this scarf off this little old woman's head and it isn't a little old woman at all, it's A. Warning, and when this scarf comes off, there she is and her hair is pink and purple and on her forehead, she's got a bright blue fringe.

"My heavens," Mrs Warren goes and claps her hand to her mouth, "whatever's Mr Kendal going to say about this?" and we didn't have long to wait till we found out because Mr K. came in then and when he saw the state of Peggy Lane's hair, he gave a very good imitation of a mad bull. Not as good as his Stan Laurel but not bad, all the same.

"Well, you just can't be in it, that's all" he says. "And to think, you've got a main part with your tambourine. What's to do now, eh? What's to do?" and Awful Warning hangs her head down and says, "Sorry, Mr K. I never thought."

"Well, that's the end of the Silver Cup for us," says Mr Kendal. "Without your tambourine, we won't be able to win that sword dancing competition and that's a fact."

Mr Kendal had us all stand stock still in a group for this sword dancing competition and we just stood there and played this very fast tune and we all had our own parts and Peggy Lane, she was supposed to be playing all the way through, as well as playing a piece on her own.

Mavis Jarvis, she marches up and clonks Awful Warning straight on top of the head. "Where's my badge?" she's shouting, "where's my badge?" and it turns out she means the badge we might have won if we'd been the best band in the sword dancing competition.

Mavis Jarvis gets to look more like a gorilla every day.

Mrs Warren, she stares at Peggy Lane and then she says, "Well, her hat will cover most of her hair and if we tuck it up, it won't show at the back."

"And her blue fringe?" Mr Kendal says. "Not to mention this 'ere safety pin through her ear."

"We'll grip the fringe up," Mrs Warren goes. "Take it right off her forehead and shove it well under the brim of her hat."

They tried this and all you could see was this blue tide mark of hair but Mr Kendal said we'd have to hope the judges didn't see it, that's all. As for the safety pin, Mrs Warren says, "That'll just have to come out," but A. Warning said it couldn't come out because if Mrs W. looked close, she'd see that P. L.'s ear was going mouldy and if anybody even breathed on this safety pin, she, P. L. would disappear straight through the Sports Centre roof.

"But it ought to come out, Peggy," Mrs Warren said when she looked at these big sores on Peggy's ear. "It looks dreadful."

Peggy Lane wouldn't even talk about taking it out but Mrs Warren said she would take her down to the hospital as soon as the band was finished otherwise her ear would drop straight off.

"As long as it don't drop off while they're playing," Mr K. snarls, and then Mrs Warren tells him off for being so heartless but this Awful Warning, they just ought to be thankful this pin isn't through her nose because she's not bothered about anything.

Pins in noses are nothing to P. L. She's got a boy friend who has his legs tied together with a bicycle chain and he can only walk about one inch at a time.

Well, what's a safety pin here or there to somebody with a boy friend like that?

By this time, we were all ready and Mrs Warren bundled old P. L.'s hair up into her hat and half of her fringe dropped back down again and Mrs Warren sighed and left it like that.

Peggy Lane looked a bit queer with half a blue fringe and a great big swollen ear stuck through with a safety pin.

"Keep close to her," Mr K. says. "Don't let anybody get a good look at her and if her ear does drop off, somebody pick it up and put it in their pocket and we'll take her down to the hospital afterwards."

And then it was time for us to go on. There were thousands of kids there, just like on the field that time.

These three big bands, they had so many kids in them, they needed practically all the hall to get their bands in. We only needed a bit of it.

We marched up and down and they marched up and down and we did all those formations Mr Kendal taught us and Deirdre Summers and her triangle weren't left over this time and Mavis Jarvis's drumstick stayed in one piece and the head didn't fly off and then it was time to play for the sword dancing competition.

"We all understand that the playing has to be very brisk," says this man into his microphone. "Very brisk indeed. This is a hard task for any band and we look forward to seeing how each individual band faces up to this highly demanding challenge."

Well, the first three bands played and nobody made any mistakes and they were very good and then it was our turn, and we faced up to the challenge all right because no sooner were we on the dance floor with these girls standing there in their kilts with swords in front of them, than there was this shouting and yelling and down the hall comes Tom, carrying his placard, and he's shouting,

"Down with children's bands," and, "Children of the World Unite. You have nothing to lose but your chains." Peggy Lane says, "He don't wanna lose his chains. Cost him money, they did." She thinks Tom's talking about her dumb boy friend and her dumb boy friend's in the dance hall and he stands up and says to Tom, "Talking to me, pal?" and he's all tied up with his bicycle chains and Tom goes push, push, and Awful Warning's boy friend falls flat on his back, on account of not being able to move his feet.

That wasn't very good and everybody started muttering about vandals and thugs and they all meant this Tom and in the end, my Gran gets him off the floor and he can't walk very well because his leg's gone stiff again and this vandal and thug has snow white hair, which just goes to show.

This Tom's moaning and groaning, "When 'e gets to my age, he won't need no bike chains on his legs. Look at this here," and he shows everybody his bad leg, "war wound that," he says, so then P. L.'s boy friend gets to be the vandal and thug instead.

Seems to me it's very handy being old sometimes.

"Right then, everybody," says the announcer. "Let's give the last band of the evening a fair hearing, right?" and there was dead silence. "All right?" shouts this bloke and this time everybody cottons on he wants them to answer, so they all shout "All right" back.

Just like at the seaside, you know.

Mr Kendal says, "Get back in your places," so we do, and then Mavis J. does a very good drum roll, which she was supposed to do, and Awful Warning of the blue hair and swollen ear, she shakes her tambourine and we're off.

I don't have all that much to do, because Mr Kendal warned me not to throw my mace up in the air for fear it came down and flattened a sword dancer.

"No chances tonight," he says, and he must have been right because none of the other bands threw their maces in the air either.

I was stood there doing this marching up and down on the spot and every now and again twirling my mace and then I looks at these sword dancers and they're getting very puffed because this is the fourth time they've danced round their swords, so I think I'll brighten things up a bit and I throw my mace as high in the air as I can.

I can hear Mr Kendal's breath going suck, suck, down his throat even over the band but I catch that mace O.K. and then I walk out in front of the band and blow my whistle and they keep playing and fall in behind me and we do a tiny march and the sword dancers keep dancing very well.

Everybody cheered and clapped and I felt smashing which was too soon altogether because Gary the Dead Beat bumped into Deirdre Collins and her triangle and sent her flying out into the middle of the sword dancers and Deirdre Collins never even blinked.

When she's playing that triangle she could be on the moon. This sword dancer bowed to Deirdre and Deirdre went ting, ting, and then the S. D. moved over and Deirdre started doing this sword dance and she did it for about two minutes before she stopped and let the girl in the kilt back again.

What an uproar that caused, but in the end we won!

Even though all the other bands shouted it was a cheat and Mavis Jarvis had to drop her drum over one of the players, splat, she went and thumped on it, we won!

Mr Kendal says, "She never stopped playing her triangle so she never cheated, no she did not." And the judges all agreed with this and then the man who made all the announcements stood up and the hall went quiet.

"The winners are . . ." and this man

stopped and smiled and Mr Kendal had three quarters of his fist in his mouth. "The winners are THE WELLY BAND!" he shouted and Mr Kendal walked up to get the Silver Cup and I went with him.

Well, we all went with him.

"Spoilt yourselves there a bit," said Mr K. after but he didn't really mind.

Stella Green got a teddy bear, special for being the mascot and she said, "T'anks, pal," because she'd heard Peggy's boy friend say 'pal' and she picks things up something terrible, their Karen says.

Mavis Jarvis got Best Drummer again, so she put two more First medals on her sash and we all got a badge each.

My Gran says it was the best night out she's had in a long time and she had a dance with Tom as well.

"Very nice too," she says.

My Mam went to the dance wearing a flower on her frock that Mr Pickle had sent her.

Then it was time to go home and Mr Kendal and his wife Mrs Warren, they were laughing and smiling all the time.

"You'll have something to put in your band book now, Lily Pickle," Mr Kendal says. And Mrs Warren (Mrs Kendal) she says, "Oh, Lily, put it all down. All about the medals and the silver cup and everything." So I have.

And about Mr Pickle.

I got this letter from him.

"Dear Lily,

Sorry I couldn't stop to see you. You know how it is. As soon as I've made my fortune, I'll be back."

Love,

Dad.

P.S. Enclosed is the 10p I borrowed from your tooth."

But I never saw him.

I never saw him at all.